# *It Sounds Familiar*

## *By S.N.Arly*

# Copyright

First Printing: 2020

ISBN: 978-0-9913209-6-7 (trade paperback)
ISBN: 978-0-9913209-7-4 (ebook)
Library of Congress Control Number: 2019920317

The Write Mann, LLC
St. Paul, MN 55106
www.TheWriteMann.com

Cover design by Shareen Mann and Beren Fox.
Cover photos by Lomig and Thierry Chabot, provided by Unsplash.

Author photo by Ben Huset, Diversicon 2018.

**Library of Congress Cataloging-in-Publication Data**

Names: S.N.Arly, author
Title: It Sounds / S.N.Arly
Description: Trade Paperback First Edition | St. Paul | The Write Mann, 2020
Identifiers:LCCN 2019920317
          ISBN: 978-0-9913209-6-7 (trade pbk)
          ISBN: 978-0-9913209-7-4 (electronic/epub)
LC record available at https://lccn.loc.gov/2019920317

# *Acknowledgments*

After many years of slowly pushing toward publication, allowing other life events and needs to bump writing to the bottom of my to do list, this book marks the first in an effort to put my writing first. This would not have been possible without the support of my family. I am grateful to my husband Steve for picking up most of the household care (and so many dinners) in September and October 2019, as I tried to complete my draft at a faster pace than I've ever written something of this length. I appreciate the willingness of my children Beren and Ranna to give up some of their usual time with me for the short term; you both inspire me to be my best self. I am thankful to our group of friends who understand that sometimes writing comes before social engagements.

I have benefited from the encouragement and constructive feedback of other writers both in the past and on this project. To the members of Guts and Rocks, Katie Ferreira & Dana Baird, thank you for plowing through something well over our word count limit to help me make this successful. Dana's knowledge of design terms and dash of reality were very helpful in this story. Extra appreciation goes to my online friend Chani who gave me a very thorough beta read on short notice when I was in dire need. If you share this with the Bear, I hope she enjoys it as much as I do.

My friends and followers on my website, Tumblr, and the Left to Write Writer's Sanctuary on Discord have been a fantastic source of motivation when days were long and enthusiasm was low. So thanks also to: Bridgetinerabbit, Emberglows, EnberLight, h-sunnywet-d, Lila the White Fox, Madtechnomage, Mama Hari, Persephoneandherhades, Raymiazaki, SunnyWet, tbehartoo, Tempomental, and youcancallmecirce for knowingly and unknowingly being the push I needed at times.

# *Fashion, French, & Mandarin Terms*

**arrondissement** – district of a large French city

**bespoke** – unique or one-of-a-kind

**boulangerie** – specialty bakery for bread

**chocolat chaud** – french style hot chocolate

**école maternelle** – equivalent to kindergarten

**haute couture** – high end fashion, custom fit and hand sewn

**hēi** (hay) – the color black

**la bise** – cheek kisses given in greeting

**le bac/Baccalauréat** – university qualifying exam

**lycée** – high school (ages 15-18)

**māo** (rhymes with ow) – cat

**mère** – mother

**patisserie** - specialty bakery for pastries

**père** - father

**première** – equivalent to junior year of high school

**prêt-à-porter** – ready-to-wear clothing

**revision** – studying for exams

**terminale** – final year of high school, equivalent to senior

# Table of Contents

## *Chapter One*

Hēi Māo sat in the very center of Brigitte's round spell rug, his eyes closed and his hands cupped together in front of him. He felt a little hiccup of excitement in his stomach instead of the anxiety that would have popped up in the past. Last year he'd been a prisoner in his father's house and subjected to magic that hurt, magic that prevented him from shape-shifting.

Now he was a familiar. Brigitte was **his** witch, and her magic felt like home. He supposed that made sense; when he'd found her, he found his true home.

*Are you ready?* Her words, like her magic, were soft and comforting, carried into his mind through their familiar bond.

*Yes.* With his past unpleasant experiences, he hadn't expected to be ready to really start learning how to use his own magic any time soon. It was so new, a power he'd only discovered when he ran away from his father seven months ago. While living on the streets of Paris as a stray cat, he'd gained rudimentary control over his magic, but he and Brigitte had been cautioned that it wasn't enough. It was well known that gaining a familiar boosted a witch's strength. Apparently the same was true for a familiar who carried their own magic.

For now, Brigitte could serve as his circuit breaker, but having seen what a magical overload looked like, he didn't want to subject her to that if it could be avoided. Before Master Fu had gone to his winter retreat near the Mediterranean, the tortoise shape-shifter had a long talk with Brigitte on the differences between witch-born and shape-shifter magic. Most of it went completely over Hēi Māo's head, but he trusted her to take care of this. She'd been nothing but wonderful to him, even when she thought he was just a cat. And he was convinced she was an arcane genius.

*Keep your eyes closed,* she said, bringing him back to the moment.

Something cold and heavy settled in his hands. Glass, maybe.

"Take a moment to just hold it and feel it," she suggested, her spoken voice a soft whisper. "You can even smell it. When you're ready, tell me what you notice about it."

After a moment, he nodded. *I've held it before.* She didn't confirm or deny. *It feels... alive?* He was pretty sure it was an inanimate object. *Does that make sense?*

*That's the magic,* she explained. *If something is used in spell casting often enough, it absorbs and holds hints of the magic it's been used for.*

He knew her magic, could recognize the steady hum of it in the red and gold rug under him. *Shouldn't it feel like **your** magic?*

"I didn't expect you to pick up on that." She let out a little huff of a laugh. "If I were the only witch-born to use it, yes. But this hasn't always been mine. My parents used it when they were teaching me, so it holds some of their magic. Our powers are complementary, so there's never been a need to cleanse it of those echoes. Everyone's magic has a distinct signature, like a fingerprint. If more than one person uses an item, the magics mix and it becomes impossible to piece out the individual signatures." Her clothes rustled a little as she adjusted how she was sitting, but she didn't move away from her spot a few feet in front of him. "What else do you feel?"

*It's not wet, but it makes me think of water... like rain or the Seine.* The river had nearly taken Brigitte's life in October. They'd been back to visit it several times, trying to create positive memories to push away the nightmares, but he doubted he'd ever love the Seine.

*Good job.* He felt the praise behind her words. *Now set it down on the rug where it seems like it fits best.*

"Anywhere?" he asked, leaning a bit to one side, trying to determine if he could feel where it was drawn to. This was similar to something he'd done a couple of times for her, helping set up her casting space or arranging her altar.

*Anywhere you can reach without getting up,* she clarified.

He held it to his left, but the vibrant sensation diminished slightly. He hovered it to his right, again feeling a drop in the subtle hum. It seemed most alive when he held it out in front of him, so he set it there.

"Very good," she said, sounding happy. "That one is keyed to the west, the guardians of water in all its forms."

He held his hands out in front of him. "Give me the next one," he said, eager to see if he could repeat his success. For so long he'd been told he wasn't worth much, that he wasn't good at anything other than serving as the face of Parenteau, his father's fashion house. His new family and his therapist had been working with him on what they called his poor self-esteem, but his drive to prove himself and help Brigitte remained his strongest motivators.

Brigitte gently placed the yellow glass disk in his hands,

smiling at his enthusiasm. By process of elimination, her clever kitty knew where it belonged, but that was only part of this exercise. "What do you feel?"

He drew in a slow breath, his closed eyelids scrunching up a bit as he concentrated. A smile broke over his face and he tilted his chin up. It was a very cat-like movement. "It's like a spring breeze." He sounded awed, as if he'd never expected to feel something like this. "It's so **real**, Brigitte."

"You like that one, don't you," she said, noticing his reluctance to put it in its obvious place behind him.

He nodded, holding it closer. "It's peaceful."

"I'm not surprised that one resonates so well with you. Air symbolizes freedom and new beginnings." She watched as he hesitantly placed it behind him. "You can open your eyes now. If you want."

The green eyes that helped make him an internationally famous model fluttered open. *That was nice.*

"You did very well." She liked seeing him so truly content. It was something that was becoming much more common the longer he was with her. "You can use these, you know." She gestured to the candle holders. "Any time you need to feel what they give you, you can take any of them out."

He gawked at her, for a moment looking far younger than his seventeen years. "I can?"

"You're my familiar, Kitty. And a familiar has the right, the exclusive right, to handle their witch's magical tools," she reminded him. There was so much he didn't know about witch-born and their relationship with both magic and their familiar. Every time she realized **just** how limited his knowledge was, she wanted to quite literally curse his father. The stupid man barely thought of his son as a person, of course he didn't think his shape-shifting son needed to know about magic.

"Handle, yes," he agreed. "But use?" He blinked a couple of times. "That seems… profane, somehow."

She shook her head. "If anyone were to use my tools without permission, it would be wrong. Their workings would be tainted, cursed actually, by the violation. But if someone has my permission, there's nothing wrong with it. With permission, it's almost as beneficial as casting magic together."

"You can do that?" he asked, leaning forward. "So… you could cast spells with Ruhul?"

She nodded. "Oh, yeah. We've done that several times." They'd been friends since *école maternelle*, and had grown up learning and doing magic together. She considered the best way to explain. Unlike a young child learning about magic, the knowledge was there; he just had the oddest gaps. "Every witch-born has their own level of power. You know that, right?"

"Yeah." He grinned. "You're super strong. My father is maybe average. On a good day."

She giggled, glad that he was finally willing to say nasty things about the man who had treated him so badly. She was far harsher in her criticism of Pierre, but she kept it to herself as much as she could. She'd been repeatedly warned to let her familiar progress toward acceptance at his own pace. She had no reason to care for the man beyond the fact that he played a small part in bringing Hēi Māo into existence.

"We also have our own strengths and weaknesses. Maman is really good with potions. Papa is better with enchantments. If they work together, they can produce some amazing potions, enchantments, and enchanted potions, which is a whole different level of magic."

"Ooooh." He was quiet for a moment, thinking. "What is your strength?"

Brigitte loved her talent, and it helped make her path in life clear, but it wasn't always the easiest to have. "Mine's a little weird. It's less straight-forward than most, so it might not make sense right away." It had been a long time since she'd had to share this with anyone. Aalia didn't even know, or if she did, she'd learned it from someone else and was tactful enough not to ask. Aalia was not really known for her tact.

*Brigitte?* He lightly pawed at her knee with two fingers. *You don't have to tell me if it makes you uncomfortable.*

She let out a sigh. "It's not that," she insisted. "You know how you sometimes feel like you're not enough?" She knew it was much stronger than that, but she tended to downplay it in hopes that he'd eventually move to a state where it wasn't so strong or frequent.

He nodded.

"I felt like that for a long time, because my magic was so different from my classmates and family." It was probably strange that he didn't know any of this yet. Bound the way they were, they needed to know each other on a much deeper level than anyone else. Since he wasn't just a cat, there was much more he could understand. "Before I started designing, we didn't really know **what** my talent was, and I couldn't understand how to use it. I felt so… inadequate." Discovering designing had been a magical epiphany.

He frowned, leaning his face closer to hers. "You're not. You know that, right?" She'd rarely seen him so serious.

"I know," she said, nodding. "But logic and emotions don't always play well together."

He snorted and settled back on his butt. "Tell me about it."

She gave herself a little shake. "My talent is creation magic. Any creation magic."

He rubbed his chin, far more vigorously than he might when checking to see if he needed to shave in the morning. "I don't understand. I mean, I've seen your magic in your designs and the clothes themselves. I saw it for the first time in my collar when you presented it to me."

"Yeah, it shows up pretty strongly in all of those."

"But doesn't that mean you should have created something to defeat the demon, like a portal? Or maybe created a serum to heal me when I blocked Celeste's curse?" he asked.

"Not necessarily." Eventually he'd understand why those were impossible solutions. "The spells I used for the demon didn't exist before I cast them," she explained. "My magic boosted them because they were literally my creations. That's also why they were so effective. If I make it, from idea to casting, my spells are more powerful than if I use a standard spell or magic process that someone taught me." She shrugged. "My grimoire is entirely unique." Most witch-born copied spells from their parents' books as they learned them, often following standards that had been in place for centuries. To take full advantage of her own talent, she'd needed to first learn those spells, then dismantle them and remake them as her own.

## *Chapter Two*

Brigitte stood with Hēi Māo at their shared locker, waiting for Aalia and Ruhul so they could go to class together. It was their usual morning routine. She looked forward to warmer weather when they could meet up on the steps outside again. While he watched for their friends, she paged through her sketch book, trying to reignite an idea she'd woken up with. It had faded the way dreams tended to, and she was sure it had the potential to be one of her best designs yet, if she could just bring it back.

She caught a sudden flicker of a reaction through the familiar bond, like concern only worse. She looked up to find Hēi Māo blocking her from students passing by. It felt intentional and more like he was guarding her than that he was trying to prevent her from getting jostled. If he'd been in cat form, she had no doubt his back would be arched and his teeth on full display.

*Are you okay?* That was a stupid question. Something had obviously upset him.

*We should get to class*, he suggested. *Aalia and Ruhul will understand if we meet them there.*

She didn't really feel like going to the room they'd be stuck in for the next three hours, but the tightness in his jaw and the stern expression frozen on his face were enough to convince her to go along with him. *Okay. You'll tell me what's wrong when we get there, right?*

He nodded, glaring at someone in a group as they moved past.

*What happened?*

He reached around her shoulders and guided her to their classroom.

Corin sat in his seat, his eyes and pen focused on the spiral book in front of him. He glanced up when they walked through the door, sending them a very casual wave with his, "good morning," before returning to his project.

He was probably working on the graphic novel he and his boyfriend started at the beginning of the year for their *première* progressive. Corin did the art while Luc handled the writing. All L'Étoile du Nord students were required to present something showing their growth over the year. Most collected a series of assignment samples as evidence of their progress, putting them together as a presentation. Others developed and presented a project of some sort. Higher scores were usually awarded to the more complex presentations, and these scores determined student priority for enrollment in the most sought after classes. Brigitte was working on a fashion line, where a different design represented each month of the school year, showcasing her skill at that point. Five months in, she could see the differences herself. Hēi Māo was still figuring out what he should present and how. Given his academic history, their teachers were quite lenient.

Brigitte put her tablet and books on the table she shared with Aalia before sitting in front of Hēi Māo on the table he shared with Ruhul. "What's wrong?" she asked. "Did something happen?"

He sighed, then shrugged, then shook his head. *There were people saying… horrible things about us in the hallway.*

She straightened up in surprise, nearly tumbling off the table. "Like what?"

He looked down at his hands, his fingers tightly locked together in his lap.

*Kitty? You can tell me. I need to know.*

*They couldn't understand why you would keep me,* he finally admitted. *They said they'd rather send their familiar away than live with a shape-shifter.* His mental voice should never sound that small and meek.

Her whole body went hot, and she suddenly understood what her mother meant when she said she was "boiling mad." It was just as well that she didn't know who'd said it, because she knew she couldn't be polite or reasonable about it. She'd probably end up suspended.

*I am **never** sending you away.* That had been one of his greatest fears when she'd learned what he was. It still came up often enough that they'd talked about it twice in their joint therapy sessions and she'd bet it was a subject in several of his individual appointments as well. *You are my familiar, and I am so grateful to have you.* She probably sounded more angry than grateful, but she couldn't help it. No one messed with her kitty's feelings.

He gave her a half smile. *I'll never get tired of hearing that.*

*How did I miss this?* She felt terribly stupid for not noticing someone bad-mouthing her familiar.

He rolled his eyes and held up one finger. *You were focused on something else. Your idea.* A second finger joined the first. *My hearing is better than yours, even in this form.*

Oh. Somehow, despite sharing close quarters with him for the past four months, she'd managed to miss that. Just because he was in his human shape, didn't mean he wasn't still a cat. She'd seen his impressive sense of smell first hand on a regular basis.

*They don't want me here.* He sounded so matter-of-fact, it needed to be addressed.

She sighed, suddenly drained and sad. *They don't want **us** here,* she pointed out. *And there will always be people like that no matter where we live.*

He nodded. While they hadn't encountered too many kids who were willing to act on their hatred toward shape-shifters, at least at school, there were some bold enough to do so. The first had been a *terminale* student, a boy from a grade ahead of them; he'd threatened Hēi Māo on his first day of school while a crowd of their peers watched and did nothing. The apparent bystander approval said much more than words could have. That boy had left school after a few weeks, bragging that his elite family was transferring him to a school that was guaranteed shifter-free.

"It's not fair," she murmured. "You don't deserve that." Couldn't they see how wonderful he was, always helping others in class and around school? He'd already had to put up with so much crap in his life.

"Why are people like that?" he asked, distress clear on his face and through their bond. "Humans and shape-shifters aren't **that** different. I've never hurt any of them."

"People are stupid," she said sadly. She'd hoped that seeing him would be enough to make people realize the rumors were lies. He was one of the sweetest and kindest people she'd ever met. The bump in his fan clubs' numbers and activities the last two months had seemed promising. But it had been naive of her to hope everything would go smoothly forever. "They'll believe the worst of others with no reason at all. I mean, in all of recorded history there's no evidence to support the belief that shape-shifters are any more dangerous than anyone else."

"Hey Gitte, Cat-dude," Ruhul said, striding into the room. He stopped so suddenly that Aalia crashed into him and Juniper, his red fox familiar, let out a sharp complaint. "What's wrong? You two look upset. Are Mama Ling and Papa Nik okay?" he asked, frowning with worry.

"They're fine," Brigitte said, shaking her head. "But I think people have gotten used to Hēi Māo enough that the gross ethnocentrism is starting to show up."

Aalia's pretty face distorted into a scowl.

*Remind me to never piss off Aalia*, Hēi Māo whispered into her mind. *She doesn't need magic to be terrifying.*

"We were warned this could happen," Brigitte said. They'd heard it from their lawyer, their therapist, and the school administration when Hēi Māo was first enrolling. She felt like she should try to calm her friends, but at the same time, she wanted them to be just as angry as she was. "Maybe we can have lunch together to do some brainstorming on how to deal with it," she suggested. "I'll ask Monsieur Levale for ideas during history."

Hēi Māo could catch about one word in seven as his witch spoke with Monsieur Levale in the hallway outside the classroom. He tried to focus on the chapter he was supposed to be reading, forcing himself to not intrude on her conversation. But it was hard. He could feel the tension as she began to shift into planning mode. He'd never met anyone who skipped fight, flight, and freeze, going straight to planning, but that seemed to be how Brigitte worked.

"Rhu?" he asked quietly.

"Yeah?" his desk mate responded, moving slightly so they could speak better without drawing attention to themselves.

"Why is Brigitte's default in a crisis to plan?" he asked.

The brown-skinned boy rubbed at his face as he thought. "Has she told you anything about her magic and the way it works?"

Hēi Māo nodded. "Is it part of her creation talent?"

Ruhul's smile was sudden, like a laugh but quiet. "That's exactly why. She **makes** solutions, and those usually need planning." He glanced out the door where she stood with the teacher, her eyes bright and her hands moving rapidly as they spoke. "They aren't always the right solutions, but she's got pretty decent luck at making solutions that are just right enough to work when they're needed."

"So she can fix this?" he asked.

Ruhul's smile faded and he turned his soft dark eyes on Hēi Māo. "I'm sorry Cat-dude, but I think changing human nature and human stupidity is beyond even her power." He reached over, hesitating for just a moment before resting his hand Hēi Māo's shoulder. He'd had the most trouble setting aside the convention that you did not touch another witch-born's familiar. "Whatever she comes up with will help, but this isn't going to be something we can fix quickly or completely. It's probably going to be something we have to deal with for the rest of our lives."

Hēi Māo nodded. He'd known that, of course. During his homeschool studies he'd learned all about history and the irrational human tendency to see differences as unbridgeable chasms. He'd overheard a thousand different jokes with shape-shifters as the punch-line, but none of them had been directed at him. Sure it hadn't felt good knowing he was the butt of a joke, but it wasn't the same as being targeted.

Growing up in Pierre Parenteau's house wasn't comfortable, so he'd always assumed this was just another version of discomfort. Dr. Wheeler kept trying to explain that his father had been abusive, that the things Hēi Māo had endured were unacceptable and even illegal. Maybe using the unpleasantness of his younger years for comparison for how people treated him wasn't the most useful.

In the end, he didn't really care what people thought of **him**.

But when they'd talked about the kinds of bias he might encounter, he hadn't realized he would be dragging Brigitte down with him. Or their friends, for that matter.

Brigitte came back in then, not smiling but definitely determined. She patted his hand as she cut close to his table on her way to the stairs. He heard her settling in to her seat and immediately getting to work. He had no doubt that she wasn't working on history. She was already creating a solution, her magic vibrating just beneath the surface of her skin.

# Chapter Three

Mama doled out sandwiches on Hēi Māo's favorite sourdough rolls before going back down to Nikli, the shop she ran with Papa. The *boulangerie patisserie* side of the business always drew a big rush over the lunch hour, while potions clientele tended to be more of a late afternoon and early evening crowd.

Brigitte was already drawing Ruhul and Aalia into her plan. She set her tablet on the end of the table to display the slide-show she'd definitely made during history class.

"So our first action needs to be, protect," she said, as the word slid in from the side of the screen.

He was going to need to make sure she ate during class breaks again, because she was completely ignoring her lunch. They'd been through that roughly once every two weeks, times when she'd spent all of lunch break working on a design she was excited about. And other occasions when she'd had to use lunch time to catch up on homework she hadn't done in favor of a design.

"Monsieur Levale said that in situations like this, a backlash is inevitable," she explained. "Anti-shifter sentiment is just too strong in France."

"Wouldn't it be inevitable anywhere?" Ruhul asked.

Brigitte shrugged. "I suppose there's a chance this wouldn't happen in New Zealand. They've elected known shape-shifters to prominent positions. It's not like a majority or anything, but there are some very strong communities there."

Hēi Māo stared at her in shock. "There are shape-shifters who don't hide what they are?" How had that never come up in conversation when they were planning his reveal on national television?

"Oh," Brigitte said, her eyes wide and her face crumpling with distress. "Yes. You didn't know that?" *I'm sorry! I'm so sorry!* "I thought you knew." Her voice was a strangled whisper.

Hēi Māo shook his head. "It's not like anyone would have told me." He sighed. Just one more thing for them both to hold against his father. "It's not your fault. You can't know what I do and don't know. There's all sorts of regular stuff I should have learned by now. And shape-shifters were a forbidden topic after Maman vanished. You know more about them... us, than I do." Sometimes they had fun working through the holes in his knowledge and experience. This was not one of those times.

"There's a huge open shape-shifter community in the United States... in, I think it's called Minnesota?" Aalia said uncertainly. "They have this intense artist scene, particularly in indie film. We should probably watch some of them..." She waved her hands when she realized she'd gotten off track. "Their situation is much more precarious than the people in New Zealand. The Americans who are out, are pretty much all living in the one state that has strong laws to protect them. But all it'll take is one really xenophobic president, and they'll have to go back into hiding. If they even can at that point."

"There are pockets in China and Japan, too," Brigitte added.

"Mostly in regions with strong folklore and culture around kind shape-shifting gods. Seven-tailed foxes, dragons, that kind of thing."

"But in Europe, the anti-shifter bias is so strong that these kinds of communities are... unimaginable," Ruhul said, his eyes reflecting sadness even more than his frown. "Until Monsieur Levale taught it last semester, it never even **occurred** to me that there might be shape-shifters in Paris. I just thought they were a really small ethnic group and they all chose to live somewhere else."

Hēi Māo slouched. Not only was this was not the positive rallying cry he was hoping for, it just highlighted how unprepared he was for the world he'd thrown himself into. Maybe he should go back to being homeschooled again. Maybe if he were out of sight, people would forget and things would die down. Ruhul and Aalia would still come visit him, right? But he couldn't let Brigitte attend school without a familiar. She needed someone to watch out for her.

"Oh, Kitty," Brigitte said sadly. "It's not that everyone feels this way. It's just that there's a really vocal minority. They're intimidating, and people don't know how to stand up to them." She slipped out of her chair and wrapped her arms around him from behind, hugging him tightly. "The backlash is a sign that those people are afraid real change can actually happen. We're at a point where that's possible. And when it happens, it'll spread, okay? We're at the toughest spot. The fulcrum of history where we can change the future. And if we can get through this we will see that change. We'll experience it."

He nodded. She was right. And **these** words gave him hope.

Ruhul let out an audible breath. He was smiling when Hēi Māo looked up again. "People should know not to tangle with Mademoiselle Butterfly's familiar. They won't know what hit them."

Aalia cackled with glee. "Give us your plan, girl. I want to see where I can fit in and how I can help. Nobody's gonna mess with our favorite cat."

Brigitte nodded, clearly relieved to have them on board.

Juniper, who had been curled up on the couch behind Hēi Māo, suddenly nosed his ankle to get his attention. When he looked down, she bounded into his lap, then scrabbled to drape herself over his shoulders. He stared across the table at Ruhul in surprise.

Ruhul grinned. "Junie's spoken, dude. We're keeping you."

Brigitte focused on outlining her plan, knowing she was going to have to come back to the multiple cans of snakes their conversations had already opened, at some later point.

"Monsieur Levale said he'd talk to the administration, let them know that we're starting to see the problems they thought would crop up." He'd promised to email her a list of the kinds of retaliation and bullying they should prepare themselves for. "I'll have a list of reportable offenses later. He's going to make us an easy report form that we can use to get complaints to the office."

"I could probably convert his form into an app," Ruhul suggested. "It wouldn't take excessive coding skills, and it would make it quick and easy."

"That's a really good idea," Aalia said, bumping his shoulder with her fist. "What can I do?"

Brigitte smiled. She was so fortunate to have these two as her best friends. "Protect includes defend. I think neither of us," she gestured to herself and Hēi Māo, "should ever be alone at school. No solo trips to the bathroom. No hitting the library on our own. We need to make sure we always have someone else who can support our claim. A witness, I guess."

"Gotta say," Ruhul growled, leaning on the table. "I'm not gonna to be one of those shitty bystanders who stands idly if someone's harassing you or my dude here." The warning was clear in his voice.

She reached over and laid her hand over his. "Thank you."

He shook his head. "No need. I will always have your back, Gitte. My friends come first."

"So if you two can't go somewhere together, one of us will be there," Aalia said firmly. "What else?"

"Our next action will be, educate." She tapped the slide-show again. "Anything we can do to teach people about shape-shifters will be helpful at this point. There are a lot of students who don't know better. They're just repeating what they've heard from family and friends, what they've seen in books and TV. We need to show them how biased and wrong that information is." While it would be nice for education to have a big impact, she doubted it would work on it's own.

"How do you educate people who don't want to know, or don't care?" Hēi Māo asked. While he looked a little less defeated than he had earlier, she missed the happiness that could radiate like sunshine off him.

"We trick them into reading or hearing the truth," Aalia said, grinning. "The more that happens, the more the message will sink in. Just leave it to me." She rubbed her hands together. "There's a reason our school paper has been nominated for so many awards this year."

"Well yeah," Ruhul said with a toothy smile. "You're freaking awesome."

"Oh stop it you." Aalia batted lightly at his shoulder, but her cheeks darkened a bit. Was she blushing? That was definitely something Brigitte would have to text her about later.

"Can't stop, won't stop," Ruhul chanted.

"Students at L'Étoile du Nord are better informed on the facts regarding current events in Paris and France than any other school in the city," Aalia said, sitting up proudly. "We draw students in with engaging headlines and topics they want to know about, and we trick them into reading facts they need to have. You see it in pretty much every article we print."

"Gee, I wonder **who** started that trend." Ruhul smirked.

"As if we didn't know," Brigitte said with a snort. Realizing her kitty didn't have the background information, she clarified for him. *Aalia introduced a very effective reporting style when she joined the school paper last year.*

"And…" Aalia's eyes were bright, a huge smile on her face. "I've just figured out an amazing *première* progressive project." She wriggled in her chair, excitement pouring off her. "Let me do some brainstorming during journalism this afternoon, and I'll report back on that. 'Kay? I want to be sure I can swing it before I get our hopes up on some big idea."

Brigitte nodded. "You have a lot of great ideas, and I'm excited to hear what you come up with." She tapped her tablet again. "Our last action is to fight back."

"Fight back?" Hēi Māo asked, his forehead furrowing.

"Not as in actual fighting," Brigitte corrected. "We need to be extra careful about violence." She'd gotten that message from both Dr. Wheeler and Monsieur Levale. "We can protect ourselves, of course, but we shouldn't ever start a fight. That'll just feed the haters. Fighting back, will be more about directly calling out hate."

"Have you ever heard the phrase, fight fire with fire?" Ruhul asked.

Hēi Māo nodded. "But I've never understood it."

"Fair deal." Ruhul shrugged. "The point is that we aren't going to just sit and let people treat you or Brigitte badly. The moment anything happens that isn't totally okay, we're going to act on it."

"We'll get started on things this afternoon," Aalia said firmly. "Should we plan to meet up here after school or will lunch tomorrow be better?"

"I'd say lunch," Ruhul suggested. "It'll give us more time to feel things out." He reached out and tapped Juniper between the eyes. "Junie's willing to do recon if we need it." The red fox slowly slipped off Hēi Māo's shoulder's to climb onto Ruhul's.

## *Chapter Four*

"Hēi Māo, Brigitte, you have company," Mama called up to the bedroom they shared.

He'd been doing his physics homework while she worked on her January *première* progressive design. "Were we expecting anyone?" he asked. They'd seen Ruhul and Aalia last night for their usual Friday game night, and he was sure Aalia said she had to babysit her sister today. When Ruhul tentatively offered to help with the babysitting, Brigitte teased both of them, causing them to blush.

He doubted Miss Gigi would stop by, and he just didn't know that many people. Brigitte had friends and acquaintances, of course, and more than a few clients commissioning her to design for them, especially now that Parenteau had started featuring her Butterfly line. But she was pretty selective about who came to the house. She preferred to meet people at cafes, and that suited him just fine.

Brigitte shook her head. "I can't imagine who it would be. But Maman wouldn't have let in just anyone." She sighed and pushed aside her sketchbook, stretching her back.

It would have been nice if it were Master Fu, but it was far too soon for that. Brigitte had done her best to understand how the overt shape-shifter hate at school made him feel, but having someone who'd been through it would really help.

Brigitte rolled her chair away from their desk, a long plank of oak mounted to the knee-wall of their attic room. It was far more rustic and comfortable than the obnoxious executive desk he'd had in his father's house. He followed her down the steps that led to the rest of the apartment. The Parenteau mansion had been large enough that the entire Defrense-Li apartment, including Nikli, would fit in the atrium of the grand entry. But it had been cold and sterile, especially after his maman left. He preferred his new cozy environment and suspected ostentatious displays of wealth would always make him uncomfortable.

A tall woman in a very fashionable blue dress stood in the living room with Mama. The woman herself seemed nervous, and an *école-maternelle*-aged boy clung to her hand looking shy. Hēi Māo didn't recall seeing either of them before.

"Hello," Brigitte said. It was a relief when he could tell that she didn't know who they were either.

"Darlings," Mama said, "this is Madame Desmarais and her son Felix. They've been regulars to Nikli since your interview." She tilted her head and opened her eyes wide in what seemed to be some sort of signal.

Unfortunately, Hēi Māo was still learning how to read human body language. He'd reliably learned when his father was about to chew him out, but that was probably more a matter of pheromones. Despite the fact that he hadn't been able to embrace his cat nature until more recently, understanding felines had come much easier.

"Oh!" Brigitte exclaimed. "I'm **so** happy to meet you." Without looking she reached back and caught Hēi Māo's hand to bring him closer. "Would you like to sit down?" She gestured to the couch. "I

23

could get some tea, or snacks."

*Who are they?* he asked, feeling like he should have been able to figure it out by now.

*Shape-shifters*, she replied. *They're here because of you.*

He stared at them in wonder for a moment, before realizing how rude he was being. "Oh, wow."

The woman's nervousness vanished, and she smiled, though it was a little sad. "Surely we're not the first cats to come meet you."

"You are, actually," Brigitte said.

"Though we have definitely seen an uptick in new clientele the last few months," Mama said, hinting. "But I'm not going to call anyone out in case it makes things dangerous for them." She nodded to their guests and then to Brigitte and Hēi Māo. "I'm going back downstairs to help Nik with the shop. Afternoon rush should be starting any moment. Call down if you need anything."

"I think we'll be fine," Brigitte insisted brightly. "So, tea? *Chocolat chaud* for our young guest?"

The little boy looked up at his mother, hopeful. "Pwease?" he asked softly.

"Brigitte makes the best *chocolat chaud*," Hēi Māo promised. "I'd never even had it before I moved here, and hers is the best."

The little boy's expression of horror made it clear he felt this deprivation was a crime.

"Okay, Felix," Madame Desmarais said, as though granting him a favor. "We can stay for a little while." She pointed to the couch. "Can you show us what a good guest you can be?"

Felix let go of his mother's hand and went straight to the couch, crawling up and sitting like a little gentleman. Brigitte let out the kind of muted squeal she made when Hēi Māo was being exceptionally cute in his cat form. And for a moment, he agreed. Felix was adorable. But then he saw himself at the same age, desperately trying to please his father, while firmly stomping out all evidence of the tendencies of small children and kittens.

Hēi Māo followed Felix to the couch, but didn't sit down right away. "Do you like to draw or play with yarn?"

"**You** play with yarn?" Felix asked, sounding surprised.

Hēi Māo nodded. "Brigitte has been teaching me to knit."

"I want to see," Felix said, his blue eyes wide and eager.

"Stay here; I'll go get it." He dashed up the stairs, quickly crossing the room to the space they'd designed as his. His bed and dresser were neatly tucked under Brigitte's lofted bed. His privacy curtains were open, as they usually were. He'd claimed they weren't necessary. Cats and models didn't need privacy, at least not like most people, and he could always use the changing screen on the other side of the room if he needed it. But Brigitte had insisted he deserved to at least have the option in case he ever wanted it. She'd also offered to let him have the bigger bed, but he didn't want it. When he'd been Jacque Parenteau, he'd had the largest possible bed, with the best mattress money could buy. He'd hated drowning in the vacuum that surrounded him. Besides, as her familiar, he could shift whenever he wanted to, and he easily spent half his nights sleeping on Brigitte's spare pillow as a cat.

He snatched up his sketch pad and colored pencils and the little basket with his current knitting. When Brigitte had caught him mindlessly kneading her skein of soft alpaca wool in human form, she'd decided he needed a human-acceptable activity for his hands. It hadn't been easy, he tended to get distracted by the dangling strands of yarn. He could do it now, and it had become almost a form of meditation.

Though he'd only been gone a moment, Brigitte and Madame Desmarais were already in the kitchen working beside the stove and getting to know each other. He sat down beside Felix, tucking his drawing supplies under the couch for later if needed. He took hold of the knitting needles and gently lifted them into the air, pulling out his latest project. Brigitte made beautiful things, following elaborate patterns that she created from thin air. He preferred to knit freestyle, casting on and throwing caution to the wind. He'd made his new family scarves, and while they weren't perfect, they were cozy, and regularly used.

"What's it?" Felix asked, his fingers twitching as he resisted the urge to reach out and touch it.

"Here," Hēi Māo said, holding it out to the boy. "When I'm having trouble sleeping, it can help me relax if I have something to squeeze." He demonstrated, digging his fingers into the stitches and clenching his hands. "That's what this will be for. So it's touchable. Squeezable."

Felix was gentle at first, before mimicking Hēi Māo's action with both hands and pulling the knit close to his cheek. "Soft." He hugged it and giggled.

Brigitte looked up from the pot of warming milk when Madame Desmarais went quiet. She followed the woman's gaze toward the living room where Hēi Māo and Felix sat together, talking quietly and laughing. Felix was apparently just as enamored of soft knit fabric as her kitty.

"Hēi Māo's only ever met one other shape-shifter besides his maman," she said. "And that's very recent. I hope you'll forgive him if he doesn't understand your cultural conventions."

Madame Desmarais nodded. "Outside of families, we have very few of those." She looked much happier than she had earlier. "When I saw your interview, I admit I was worried for him. He seemed content, so I knew you were treating him well, but it was clear he was still missing something. He'd gone out in search of shape-shifters, and hadn't found any." She turned back to Brigitte but wouldn't meet her eyes. "**We** should have been looking for him."

The unevenness in her voice spoke of shame.

Brigitte shrugged. "There was no way for you to know what he was, or what he was looking for." She carefully poured the chopped chunks of chocolate into the hot milk, whisking as she went.

"That's not entirely true." Madame Desmarais shook her head. "His mother was well known, particularly among cats. When she disappeared, several people I know tried to get close to Jacque Parenteau. They merely wanted to see if he needed anything we could offer, to create a connection if he wanted it. But even before he became a world famous model, his father's security detail was far too good." She frowned, her whole manner drooping a little. "When news went out that Jacque had gone missing from a photo shoot, we all knew he'd run away. Of course that's what he'd done, and **we** should have been looking for him. He shouldn't have needed to spend months living on scraps, trying to find us."

"There's no guarantee you would have found him," Brigitte said. "He was extremely vigilant, skittish, even."

"**You** managed to find him," Madame Desmarais said, not quite accusing.

Brigitte smiled and shook her head. "No. He found me."

"So that part of the story is true?" she asked, clearly surprised.

"It means a lot to me that he chose me," Brigitte explained. "Even when I thought he was just a very clever cat, that was important." Every time she'd inquired of her magic how she should go about finding a familiar, it had been very clear that it wanted a free animal, one who chose the life. "Can you see chi patterns, Madame Desmarais?" Master Fu made it sound like a universal shape-shifter talent but Hēi Māo hadn't had any success figuring it out on his own yet.

The woman nodded.

"I can't see them myself, but Maman and one of our mentors can, and they've said we are a good match." She couldn't stand the idea of other shape-shifters thinking she'd tricked or trapped Hēi Māo into staying with her or becoming her familiar. If he truly wanted to leave her, she'd let him, though it would hurt more than anything she could possibly imagine. "I'm not the kind of witch who owns her familiar. Now that he's in my life, his happiness is as important as my own."

## *Chapter Five*

Aalia and Ruhul met Brigitte and Hēi Māo at the cafe directly across from L'Étoile du Nord. It was their new morning routine, ensuring no one could single them out once they got to school. Being in a group made it harder for people to gang up on them. Together, they arrived early enough to go to all their lockers as a group.

Brigitte tried to focus on the positives. It was nice to start the cold winter days with a warm drink, and they'd always liked visiting with each other before class. They could touch on homework problems or discuss whatever they were binge watching at the moment. Ruhul had introduced her to more than one truly fantastic anime, after all.

The locker she and Hēi Māo shared was closest to their primary classroom, so it was always last. As they approached their bank of lockers, Brigitte noticed a large number of fliers stuck to the front of one of them. As they got closer, she realized it was theirs. Certain it was a bit of nastiness, she stepped to the front of their little pack, yanking all the papers off once she was within reach.

There was nothing really wrong with the poster, which cautioned students against plagiarism. But seeing what looked like the entire school's worth of fliers, concentrated on the shape-shifter's locker, made the message abundantly clear.

Scowling, she shoved them into her bag and turned to Aalia. "I've got your next Take Shape topic," she said, referring to the series her friend had started the week before. It had served as her launching point for *Miraculous Morph*, the blog-heavy website she planned to use as her *première* progressive. She was running some of her shorter articles in the school's weekly newspaper, but even more were going up on her site.

Aalia frowned, as she ran her hand over the metal door to peel off any missed tape. "What is it?"

"It seems that some people still think that shape-shifters can turn into anyone or anything." She was hoping *Miraculous Morph* would help them spread the education effort to more people, but they were still early in building a following.

Aalia nodded. "It was on my list of ideas. I'll just bump it up to the top."

Ruhul held out his hand. "Give me the posters, Gitte. I'll handle this one."

"Are you sure?" Brigitte asked. They'd been taking turns submitting complaints to school administration with Ruhul's app. She didn't keep track of numbers, that was Ruhul's job, but she was reasonably sure she hadn't needed to submit more than a quarter of them. She wasn't convinced the school was really doing all it could to address the problem, but it was still too early to lodge that complaint.

Ruhul nodded. "I added an attachment option to the app," he explained. "I want to test it, make sure it works. And those fliers would be perfect for it."

"I could do it," Hēi Māo suggested.

"Sorry, Cat-dude, but that's not happening," Ruhul said. "We've got your back."

Hēi Māo frowned, and his eyes looked sad. "But you shouldn't have to do this."

Ruhul opened his mouth to speak, but Juniper let out a shrill growl of irritation. He smiled, and scratched behind her ears before translating for those who couldn't understand. "She wants to bite their faces off for you."

Hēi Māo's green eyes had gone wide and he let out a startled laugh. "Thank you, Juniper."

"I know this is tough for you to understand, coming from the kind of place you grew up, but we **want** to do this for you," Ruhul said. "You're one of my very best friends. It's hard seeing people be nasty to you, and there's no way I'm letting you put up with it on your own." He let out a huff, sounding a bit like his familiar. "There are going to be times I won't be there or won't be able to pick this up for you. So when I can, just let me. Okay?"

Brigitte handed the crumpled heap  them to Ruhul. She didn't like how withdrawn Hēi Māo had become in the last few days. She wondered if he needed to see Dr. Wheeler ahead of schedule or if a visit with Madame Desmarais and Felix would help. Meeting other cat shape-shifters had definitely been a mood lifter.

"You belong here with us," she said firmly. "And anyone who says otherwise is wrong."

Finding the posters on their locker made Hēi Māo feel like turning cat and never coming back to school in his human form. But it got better after that and the morning seemed on track to be relatively uneventful. No one had tried to trip him in the hallway, though that might have been because no one could get close enough to do so. It would have been funny to let them try. It was a well known truth that cats didn't trip, and few people knew that cat shape-shifters didn't either.

He wondered if it was too much to hope that they would get through the last two days of school before winter break without any other awful things happening.

"All right," Monsieur Lavale called their history class to order. "Who has a current events topic for us to discuss?" Since they had just finished up a unit, and wouldn't be starting a new one until after the break, he'd announced they would spend one day discussing current events and the other on historic events that continue to impact the modern era.

From his spot at the front of the room, Hēi Māo heard several of his classmates move as they raised their hands. He turned his head and saw Aalia's fingers reaching for the ceiling.

"Alexa," Monsieur Lavale said, gesturing to a girl in the back row. "What do you have for us today?"

"Tariffs on plants imported from China," she suggested.

The history teacher looked impressed, and nodded his head once. "Excellent choice. It has an impact on a lot of students. Do you want to get us started?"

The class discussed what they understood about the recently imposed tariffs and the reasons government officials gave for implementing them. Once the topic was exhausted, Monsieur Lavale made some suggestions for further research if anyone was interested in taking action or learning more. Then he took the next topic. Lucie brought up the recent age and body fat index regulations for models in French shows. Corin shared the French Heritage Society's appeal for funding for restoration projects at multiple historic sites in Paris. As Monsieur Lavale moved through the class, some issues were more relevant to witch-born, but most were applicable to all of them. Students didn't always agree, and Hēi Māo was impressed how well they handled the difference in opinions.

Hēi Māo had been aware of some of the news and events his classmates had brought up, but he hadn't quite gotten the hang of regularly watching the news or reading the papers online. It wasn't something he'd been allowed to do when living with his father. Now that media was accessible to him, it was easy to get overwhelmed by the sheer volume of information. He was still trying to figure out which sources were reliable, and which ones were the kind of thing Pierre Parenteau had claimed to be protecting his son from.

"Okay, we have time for one more topic," Monsieur Lavale said, clapping his hands together twice as they wrapped up a vigorous conversation related to the pollution in the Seine. "Simon, what is your topic?"

"I've heard some serious concerns about the use of shape-shifters as familiars," Simon said.

Hēi Māo's stomach felt like it was full of rocks, heavy and uncomfortable.

Their teacher's eyes narrowed slightly. "We're looking for actual news, Simon, not gossip."

"You can't tell me this isn't news," Simon said dismissively. "I hear about it in the hallways here at school, from my family at the dinner table, and in discussion groups online."

"Ethnophobic hate groups," Aalia snapped.

"Trying to silence me doesn't make it any less important or true," Simon said smugly.

"This isn't about silencing anyone," Monsieur Lavale said firmly. "I've been pretty clear that I expect you all to have and use your own minds. But you seem to have forgotten that respect is a necessary element to that equation."

"I'm not disrespecting anyone," Simon insisted, one hand on his chest. Hēi Māo did not buy his implied sincerity, and he wondered if anyone in the class really did.

"Simon." Monsieur Levale's eyebrows had raised, and his expression was disappointed. The black and white border collie that accompanied him to class every day abruptly sat up in the dog bed at the corner of the room. "As there's only one known shape-shifter familiar in the **world**, and the issue hasn't made an appearance in **any** of the major media outlets, your topic is clearly ad hominem. I suspect Aalia is correct that your discussion groups are not exactly reputable sources. That makes your topic hearsay or rumor rather than news."

"So you're saying you're fine with slavery, then?" Simon demanded. "Allowing any one group to have that kind of power over another... that's what it is. Call them familiars, or call them slaves. It's all the same." He shrugged again. "And once the shape-shifters are under their power, who's to say they won't come after other groups of non-witch-born?"

There was a moment of silence before the class exploded in an uproar. Familiars were as loud, or in some cases louder than their witch-born partners.

"You have no idea what you're talking about!"

"Idiot!"

"Familiars aren't slaves, even when they're regular animals," Ruhul snapped. One hand attempted to soothe Juniper, who had both front feet planted firmly in his black hair while she shrieked at Simon.

Hēi Māo raised his hand, pretending that the ruckus around him didn't exist. As his classmates realized he was waiting, they gradually went quiet. **He** was exclusively qualified to address Simon's claims.

"Yes, Tom," Monsieur Lavale said, turning to him. "Did you have something you wanted to add?"

Hēi Māo nodded. "It's true that many familiars didn't choose their lives, honestly most are incapable of understanding what

34

they're being considered for until they've been elevated. But I've never met one who regretted it, and I've spoken with a lot of familiars in the last six months."

"You can speak with other familiars?" Monsieur Lavale asked, surprised.

Hēi Māo nodded. "It's easier when I'm a cat, but all familiars can understand each other. It's part of the familiar magic." He turned and looked at Simon. "It's not your culture, so you can't possibly begin to understand how wrong you are." He was pleased to see that prompt a reaction from the other boy who had been posturing as calm and concerned. "Make no mistake, I **chose** to become a familiar. And I specifically chose Brigitte as my witch. When we came out of the familiar ceremony, I had fewer bonds than when we started, but she had more." She was as bound to him as he was to her. "Familiar partnerships are not one-sided. Your concern and your argument are fundamentally flawed."

Monsieur Levale nodded, then turned to the class. "All right. We're going to wrap up here." He pointed at Simon. "Simon, I need you to stay after for a few minutes." He looked at Brigitte and then Hēi Māo. "Can you two come to my office after last hour?"

Hēi Māo nodded, knowing Brigitte would be willing. Monsieur Lavale had been one of their strongest sources of support and guidance. If he wanted to talk to them, they would make the time.

Hēi Māo watched as Ruhul and Brigitte made lunch and Aalia paced through the living room. Juniper had curled up in his lap after assuring him that he was the best boy, aside from her Ruhul, of course. He felt oddly calm, maybe a little disconnected from everything that was going on.

"What a complete and utter asshole," Aalia mumbled. "I'm so concerned for the poor shape-shifters," she said in a simpering falsetto. "Oh, no, the witch-born will come for us all. Asshole."

*Is Aalia okay?* he asked.

Brigitte glanced up, took in their friend, then shot him a small smile. *She's seething. Don't worry. She'll get it out of her system and come back strong. She's good like that.*

Ruhul lifted the pot he'd been tending off the stove. "Soup's ready. I think I got it hot enough without going too hot this time."

"Good," Brigitte said, patting his shoulder. "I like to keep the skin on my lips and the roof of my mouth." She pulled a sealed bowl out of the refrigerator. "Juniper, do you want some chicken?"

Juniper called back, "Chicken and eggs are always good," making Hēi Māo snicker even as Ruhul was translating for his familiar.

"He's jealous," Aalia said suddenly. Hēi Māo realized she'd stopped pacing. "He wishes he had magic, and he's jealous of yours." She frowned in thought. "And he might be a little bit afraid of you, probably because he's a guy who can't handle the idea of strong women."

"I'd say you got it in one," Ruhul said. "That sums him up pretty well."

"Education isn't going to be enough for jerks like him," Aalia said, crossing the room to take a seat beside Hēi Māo. "We need to do more than that."

"Like what?" Brigitte asked, dismay clear on her face.

Aalia grinned, and it looked downright feral. "People at school have gotten used to the idea that Hēi Māo is a shape-shifter, but out in the rest of Paris, it's still pretty new. They don't see him on the daily."

"Go on," Ruhul encouraged.

"Before the rest of Paris can join in on the hate bandwagon, I'm going to expand *Miraculous Morph*," Aalia explained, rubbing her hands together in excitement. "It's the best platform we have available, so I'm going to need all three of you to do anything you can but haven't already, to signal boost. We're no longer just targeting kids our age," she clarified. "I'm going to go way beyond little articles on the history of shape-shifters and debunking myths. I'm going to control the narrative. I'm going to have interviews... documentaries... oh my gods this is going to be **so** awesome."

"Won't that take up a lot of time?" Hēi Māo asked, she was already using her skills and energy for him. He hated to think of her giving up too much of her free time.

"Don't you worry, Cat-dude," Aalia said. "This is as much for me as it is for you. This will give me an excellent *première* progressive score while also launching my journalism career outside the realm of the *lycée*. And as a bonus, it'll be great for my portfolio for university or job searching." She grinned in satisfaction.

Brigitte patted his hand. "And this is how we come back strong."

# Chapter Six

Hēi Māo woke abruptly. He was in cat form on Brigitte's pillow and the room was dark. He sat completely still, sniffing the air and listening. He never just woke up like that. Surely something had woken him. The apartment was quiet. He closed his eyes and focused on the shop below.

He growled when he picked up a scraping sound. *Brigitte. Wake up.* He nudged her with one paw.

"Hmmm?" she mumbled. "Wha's wrong, Kitty?"

*I think there's someone outside Nikli.* He glanced at the alarm clock. There was no good reason for someone to be lingering outside a closed shop at three in the morning. He shifted so he could push open the trapdoor in her ceiling, leading to a patio on the roof. He climbed up, moving as silently as he would have in his other form. This was one of those times when it was really good to be a cat. Careful to stay back in the shadows, he peered over the railing. There were three men on the sidewalk at the front of Nikli. They had a toolbox and several cans of spray paint.

How dare they? This was his witch's home. Her family

business. How dare they profane it with their hate. *Call the police. Wake up Papa.*

He heard Brigitte scramble out of bed. *What's happening?*

*There's three men defacing the front of the shop.* Crouching low on the balcony, he shifted again, hoping they couldn't see the faint flash of green light. He moved to the fire escape, working his way down to the second-floor window ledge just above the men.

*What are you doing?* Brigitte asked. *Papa says you need to get back in the house. We don't want you to get hurt.*

*I can't just ignore them. And they might get away.* There was no way he was going to allow that.

*Where are you?* she demanded.

*I'm over the front windows,* he explained. *Just watching. If someone comes out from the alley, we can take them down.*

*Wait for my signal,* Brigitte cautioned. *Do not attack unless I'm there.*

He sighed. He'd rather Papa or Mama came to help him. He didn't like Brigitte being in danger, and while she was amazing in a magical fight, he had no idea how she could handle herself in a physical one. He'd been in cat fights. He'd trained in karate, since it kept him fit and served as good self-defense. It was her home, too, though. So he really couldn't blame her for wanting to handle it.

"Fucking filthy shape-shifters," one of the men mumbled. "Can you believe it had the audacity to show up on the news acting like it belonged here."

"Well this should send the right message," another responded. There was more scraping, suddenly followed by the distinct rattle of a metal ball mixing up paint.

Hēi Māo flinched when he heard the hissing of the spray can. No, no, no. Why couldn't he have heard them **before** they damaged his family's home and business. He was so overwhelmed by guilt, he missed hearing the alley door open and the soft footsteps that followed.

"What **exactly** are you doing to my shop?" Mama demanded.

He was relieved it wasn't Brigitte standing down there, but he would have preferred the imposing visage of Papa, an absolute giant of a Frenchman.

The men laughed derisively. "You called this on yourself," one of them said.

"Harboring a shape-shifter," another sneered. "Trying to make it sound perfectly safe and normal." He spit on the ground.

"Makes me think you haven't truly assimilated to French culture, **foreigner**," the first said, making the last word sound disgusting.

Mama was a tiny Chinese woman, the shortest person in the house, and she looked so vulnerable standing on the faintly lit corner, holding nothing but a broom. "You seem to have forgotten an important detail," she pointed out. "Everyone in this home has some form of magic."

His vision went oddly blurry, like he'd gotten water in his eyes. He blinked a couple of times, and the impression that Mama was fragile, faded. Before he could truly consider what this meant, he felt a light magical draw from Brigitte. She was up on the roof, and when he closed his eyes it was almost like he could see her casting her circle. She was walking widdershins this time, something his father had often done. But he'd never seen her do it. Did it mean something?

*See if you can drop a bit of bad luck on them,* Brigitte suggested.

He'd been prepared to pounce on them, biting and scratching, but she was right. Keeping a distance made sense. He held out his right front paw and closed his eyes. Focusing on his magic, something he could now find inside himself, thanks to his practice sessions with his witch. It felt like it looked, dark and sparkly, all sharp edges and destruction. He waved his paw over the men, watching with satisfaction as the curse hit where he'd aimed, and things started going wrong for them.

Brigitte stood in the center of the tiny circle she'd called up. She wore only a t-shirt and a loose pair of flannel pants, and the mid-February air lay cold and damp against her skin. The moment she felt Hēi Māo's magic disperse, it was her turn. "Guardians of earth," she whispered, reaching out to the north. "Protect the business that helps my family thrive." She swung her hand to the east. "Guardians of air, masters of freedom, aid me in temporarily denying freedom to those who would harm my loved ones." She pushed away, as though batting at a fly.

The men shouted, one screamed. She could vaguely hear her maman talking, but it didn't carry over the noise of the men who'd found themselves trapped, unable to move. Good. They deserved to panic and fear for choosing to inflict those same feelings on her family.

She held up a tiny twig. "Upon breaking this stick, let the binding dissolve." The twig glowed for a moment. "Blessings upon you guardians. I give thanks for your assistance this night." She closed her eyes again, dropping her arms and her circle at the same time.

She put the spell breaker in her pocket and gave herself a little shake before ducking back into her room. She half-slid down the ladder, then the stairs so she could reach the living room window where her familiar sat. She pushed the casement up, and urgently picked at the screen latches.

Hēi Māo's luminous green eyes gazed at her through the screen, but the rest of his features were lost in the shadows.

"You're such a good kitty," she murmured.

"Nicely done, Cupcake," Papa said from behind her. He held a phone to his ear while Callie circled his feet nervously. "Come back in, Son." He looked through the screen at her familiar. "The police are on their way. Between the two of you magicking them, and Ling down there, this mess is as good as over."

Hēi Māo glanced over the ledge one last time before slipping through the window. He shifted back while Brigitte restored the screen and pulled the window closed. Only then did she let out a massive shiver that was as much for the cold as the adrenalin rush.

"They damaged Nikli's storefront," Hēi Māo said, distress clear in his voice.

Papa nodded, then moved closer and wrapped her familiar in a hug. "Vandalism is the act of scared and petty people, Son. We have insurance, and no one was harmed. That's what matters."

Brigitte heard the sirens screaming down the street.

"You two stay up here, I'm going to go help Ling talk to the police." Papa gestured to the couch.

"Oh. Do you want the spell breaker?" Brigitte pulled the stick out of her pocket.

"Will your spell prevent the police from hauling them away?" Papa asked.

She nodded. "They're frozen, not with cold or ice. Just stuck in place."

Papa nodded, gently wrapping his big fingers around the stick. "Nice choice, Cupcake. Less harmful than you'd have been within your rights to be. They were attacking your home after all."

She dropped to the couch and let out a sigh. While she'd known that people were willing to do this sort of thing, she hadn't really expected to see it happen. Especially not so soon. She wasn't ready for it. To be fair, she would probably never be ready for it.

Hēi Māo paced around the room, a restless cat in human form. He paused to lean toward the window, then continued on, occasionally returning to gaze toward the street below.

"Kitty?" she asked, worried. It was as if he'd tucked his feelings into a locked box, and she couldn't tell if he was nervous, angry, scared, or something else.

"I know..." he said softly. "Papa said insurance will fix it." He looked out the window again. "But there's more to it."

"What do you mean?" Did he feel guilty? None of this was his fault; surely he knew that. Right?

He stopped and looked at her, his face slack and his eyes haunted. "This could have been worse." He swallowed. "If this is how it starts, how bad will it have to get before it gets better?" He looked away, but not before she saw the shimmer of tears in his eyes. "What if it's a fire next time? What if someone gets hurt?"

She heard full well the words he wasn't saying. What if one of them dies? She held her arms open to him, and he rushed to hug her. She pulled his head to her shoulder so she could run her fingers through his hair. It soothed human him as much as it did cat him.

"After Maman lost Xīng, she and Papa protected the shop and our home," she whispered. They hadn't spoken much about her maman's original familiar, so of she hadn't told him this before. "We reinforce the protections every three months, on the high holidays."

"It didn't stop those men," Hēi Māo said, shaking his head, but not pulling away.

"No, it didn't." He had a point, and she needed to consider how to address it. "But explosives are extinguished the moment they touch the property, and harmful fire can not find purchase, even in the old wood floors and supports."

He relaxed a little.

"But you've brought up something we should definitely think about," she said. "We need to work on providing better protection both here and when we're out and about. You're internationally

43

famous and people **do** recognize you." She sighed, knowing this was going to need to be her top priority over winter break. "We can figure this out."

## Chapter Seven

Brigitte closed the curtains so she wouldn't have to see the news van parked on the opposite corner from Nikli. The crew stood in the street, filming Nala Freis as she reported on the attack. Brigitte didn't need the reminder of the ugly markings to the woodwork and glass, and she worried about how her familiar was handling all this. He'd been too miserable to speak at all when the police interviewed her last night, staying cat and snuggling restlessly in his sling. He'd done the same when the prefect of police visited early this morning and formally requested permission to add Brigitte's binding spell to the police force's grimoire.

"Are they going to be able to open at all today?" Hēi Māo asked, peeking out the living room window before stepping back.

"After the insurance team gets out and takes pictures, we'll be able to cover it up with a tarp… or we might leave the damage as is and just open the shop," Brigitte explained. He hadn't even had the most basic understanding of how insurance worked, and she'd heard Maman explaining before she went down to prep for today's preorder pick-ups.

"Why would they leave it for people to see?" Hēi Māo asked, his face twisted in revulsion.

"So people know what happened and that we're not afraid," she explained. "So those who aren't familiar with Nikli know that we are willing to face this in support of shape-shifters." He was still so new to her family and how they did things. "Now come eat your breakfast. You'll need your energy when Ruhul gets here."

Hēi Māo shrugged. "I'm not very hungry."

She frowned. "That's your emotions talking." She patted the table. "Come on, Kitty. Ruhul and I are going to be casting lots of big stuff today, which means I'll need my familiar charged up and ready to help."

"What exactly are you and Ruhul doing?" he asked. He'd been sulking in bed when she was on the phone so he hadn't even gotten her side of the conversation.

"We're going to put some magic in our clothes, specifically yours and mine to repel harm." She paused for a moment. Aalia and Ruhul were at just as much risk for being targeted. Aalia's website had taken off, picking up hundreds of new followers a day once Tom Hēi mentioned it on his social media. Her parents were also in danger as vocal supporters of shape-shifters. Though she hadn't seen it yet, they'd told her they were going to talk to Nala when she showed up. Their planned message was to reiterate their support despite the obvious hate crime.

"What's wrong?" he asked, coming to sit at the table.

"I think we need to change our plan for the spell, maybe use an agent so we can distribute it wider." Instead of putting the magic directly on the clothes, perhaps if they put it in a detergent, they could apply it to anyone's clothes. "A spray," she muttered.

"A what?" Hēi Māo asked.

"If we put it in a spray, we can get it on all of Aalia and Ruhul's clothes too. And my parents'. Bonus for us that we wouldn't have to put the clothes in the center of the working." That would be a mess. Getting everything put away again, or casting the spell multiple times at each home. She nodded. A spray was totally the new plan.

"Did you just invent a new spell," Hēi Māo asked, the first smile of the day finally appearing on his face, tentative and soft.

She shrugged. "I was planning on creating something new when Ruhul gets here, but now I have an even newer plan."

"You look happy when you create things," he said. "It's nice."

"Thank you." It was a little embarrassing, but also kind of sweet to hear that. "It does make me happy."

He leaned over and twitched the curtains to glance out the window near the table. "The news truck's gone."

"They got their scoop…"

"Maybe Aalia should come over and get some pictures for *Miraculous Morph*," Hēi Māo suggested. "We know she won't sensationalize it."

"That's **just** what I was thinking." She smiled at him. It was nice when they were in synch like that. She was just finishing making their breakfast, omelets packed with ham and spinach. "Can you text her? I mean, she knows what happened. I already told her that. But maybe ask if she wants us to get pictures for her?"

Hēi Māo slid his phone out of his pocket. He insisted he didn't need it, and strictly speaking, that was probably true. He preferred to stay with Brigitte, and she could hear him no matter where he was. But she'd agreed with her parents that he should have his own. Mama and Papa wanted him to understand that he was his own person and should have his own things and his own life, even if it was connected to hers. They often sent texts over lunch when Brigitte and Hēi Māo went to cafes or friends' houses. Brigitte usually got the messages to pick up milk or butter; he got reminders of appointments and affection.

She smiled, watching his finger glide over the screen. Though he'd resisted at first, he clearly enjoyed having his own phone. He was adapting well to the technologies and freedoms his father had kept from him.

His phone blooped at him, announcing three incoming messages in rapid succession. They were all from Aalia. "She's getting dressed right now." He looked up at Brigitte. "Is there any reason she can't stay for the casting?"

Brigitte shook her head. "That's a good idea, actually. She hasn't gotten to see a lot of magic, and she finds it fascinating."

"Then she could take her spray home and use it tonight," he suggested.

He looked back down at the screen and wrote another text asking her to stay after she's done with the pictures. She could work on her own thing while Brigitte and Ruhul planned their spell or spells. It could be like when they all got together to work on homework or to study for a test. He'd gotten to do all of these things recently and enjoyed the idea that he could be productive and working without isolating himself from others.

Hēi Māo carried Brigitte's altar to its place in the center of the round rug. She and Ruhul sat at her desk discussing the finer details of her plan.

"I wish I had fingers," Juniper said, her whine soft in his ear from where she perched on his shoulder.

"I can't imagine the mischief you'd cause," Hēi Māo said with a smile. "Besides, you're a lovely fox. Fingers would spoil the look."

She poked her nose in his ear, something she did when he or Ruhul irritated her. "I can't set up his casting space." She looked around at the work they'd done, more that he'd done while she

48

supported.

"You could help with the candles," he suggested. "They're light and you've got a gentle mouth."

She perked up. "Yes. Let me help with them."

"And maybe we can redesign some of Ruhul's tools so you can help him more," he said. "If it's what you really want." He strode back to the chest and pulled out the box of fat white candles. "Do you know where they go?"

Juniper hopped down and sniffed the candles once, letting out a tiny sneeze. "Yes." She withdrew one and danced over to one of the candle holders. "West, yes?"

"Good job." He pulled the others out and set them where she could easily reach them. "You take care of those while –" He broke off when he heard sounds down in the apartment. A moment later, there were footsteps charging up the stairs. He moved, ready to intercept if needed.

"Guys!" Aalia gasped, as she appeared through the trapdoor. "Did you see?"

"See what?" Brigitte asked.

Aalia ran to the window and opened the curtains. "Look, look, look!" She pointed vigorously, then turned and beamed at all of them. There was a construction crew gathered on the sidewalk.

"Wow," Brigitte said. "I didn't think Maman and Papa had even had a chance to call a contractor yet."

"They haven't!" Aalia bounced up and down. "They're all shape-shifters or shifter supporters. They just showed up without warning, and they're here to fix the damage. For free."

Hēi Māo's eyes suddenly stung. He pressed a hand to the window to peer down at the group. They carried toolboxes and pushed carts. They were dressed to work. "Why?" he asked quietly. "Why would they do this?"

He abruptly found himself in the center of a group hug.

"They want to help you, Hēi Māo," Aalia said. "You coming out publicly, completely unashamed of what you are has been important to them. It's how you should all be able to be."

"How do you know all this?" Brigitte asked as her hand slipped into his hair, immediately soothing him.

"I was downstairs when they came," Aalia explained, still a bit breathless. "I talked to some of them about you two, the vandalism, and *Miraculous Morph*." She stepped back to spin in a happy circle. "Some of them are going to check it out, and if they like what they see, they'll let me interview them. No photos or identifiers, of course. But this is an amazing opportunity. It's going to ensure I'm including the population I'm speaking out on behalf of."

"Those assholes did a lot of damage," Ruhul said. "They really gouged up the woodwork, and I'm sure the paint is never coming off the windows."

Aalia nodded. "They have glass specialists and woodworkers. They're working under one woman who has a renovation business, and they'll cover anything the insurance doesn't."

Why did their kindness make his chest hurt? "I think we should… Can we thank them?" he asked quietly, struggling to get the words out right.

Brigitte took his hand, squeezing it gently. "I think we should."

The shop was busy when Brigitte peeked in, far busier than usual, actually. She wondered if their regulars had come en masse to show their support, or if there were new customers doing that. Hēi Māo held tightly to her hand as they went out the back way, into the alley. The same door Maman had used last night. *It's okay to be nervous,* she told him. He seemed both eager and reluctant to meet the construction crew.

He glanced at her, sheepish, and shrugged. *I've hardly ever met any shape-shifters. What if they don't like me.*

She knew there was more to it than that.

*What if I'm not good enough for them?*

She couldn't promise they'd all be nice people, and that they'd like him. Assuring him that he'd be good enough felt artificial, and she couldn't do that to him. *I don't think they'd be here if that was an issue.*

Aalia and Ruhul had gone ahead of them. Since she'd already talked to the woman coordinating the work, she could help with introductions and maybe break the ice a bit.

"Would you rather meet them in the apartment?" she asked. "I'm sure some of them could come up."

He stiffly shook his head. "I'm not comfortable with strangers coming into our demesne."

She grinned at him. "You're territorial."

His green eyes rolled upward. "I **am** a cat, you know. That doesn't just stop when I'm human."

"I promise that's a detail I am unlikely to forget." He'd taken great joy in being able to present in whichever shape he felt like when they were at home. She liked waking up to him sprawled over the pillow beside her, and she still took her sling everywhere in case he wanted to shift. Paris could be overwhelmingly busy, even when you were accustomed to the concentration of people and bikes and cars. He'd spent most of his life locked away from it.

"I feel like I'm being a scaredy-cat right now," he said with a half smile.

"Pfft!" She laughed. He'd found a love for puns while hanging out with Papa. "You're cautious, and that's okay. You've been hurt by people before."

"Here they come," Aalia said, peeking around the corner and leading a tall woman with a light brown bangs peeking out from under her hardhat. "Brigitte, Tom, this is Esmée Travers. She's the brains behind the volunteer effort to fix the damage."

"It's a pleasure to meet you, Madame Travers," Hēi Māo said, nodding to her.

"I can't tell you how much we appreciate your help," Brigitte said. She knew she shouldn't be curious about what kind of animal the woman could shift into, but the thought couldn't be stomped down.

"Please call me Esmée." Her smile was warm and welcoming. "And it's the least we can do for those who stand up for our rights." She reached out with both hands, to capture Brigitte's. "I'm afraid this is just the start of what you'll have to endure, as Paris shows you the ugly side of her face."

Brigitte nodded, feeling like she'd been given both a warning and an apology. "I know. We've been expecting it, well… not this specifically, but problems in general."

Esmée squeezed her hands then reached for Hēi Māo's. "May I?" She quickly met Brigitte's eyes and then his.

*It's your choice,* Brigitte reminded him when he hesitated. *It's always your choice to let people touch you or not.*

He nodded, offering his hands to Esmée.

"Your life has not been easy, Tom," she said softly. "And while most of us are unable to be as bold and public as you are, we are here for you." Her smile was rueful. "You have the harder part, convincing the world that we aren't a threat. And I am personally grateful that you're willing to do this." She released his hands.

"We kind of had to," he said, reaching back to rub at his neck. Her poor kitty wasn't used to praise. He wasn't sure what to do with it. "It was going to get out eventually. And Brigitte wanted me to have all the opportunities available to people, if I wanted them."

"Esmée!" a man called. "We need you to take a look at –" His voice cut out as he moved to see who she was talking to. "Oh. Hello. Sorry to intrude."

"Not at all," Brigitte said quickly. "We're the ones interfering with your work. We really just wanted to come thank you all."

The man grinned at them. "No thanks needed, Mademoiselle Butterfly."

"We'll speak later," Esmée promised. "Your parents have invited us all to an appreciation dinner once our work is done."

"Oh," Hēi Māo said softly. "That's wonderful. I really don't want to get in the way of your work, but I do want to thank everyone."

"You may want to prepare to take a few selfies and sign a few autographs then," the man suggested with a smile. "More than a few of us have family who are big fans of your work."

Brigitte giggled. *Are you willing to do that?*

Hēi Māo nodded. "We can definitely do that."

## *Chapter Eight*

Hēi Māo lounged in his hammock, idly watching Brigitte as she sketched. She'd gotten some fantastic new idea over lunch, but she hadn't been ready to share it just yet. She'd gone through several pages already, and while he could see the frantic sweep of her pencil slowing down, he suspected there was much more to come from this latest brainstorm of hers.

She closed the sketchbook and set it aside. *Are you done already?* he asked, surprised.

She smiled and shook her head. "Just for the moment. I need to let the idea percolate a little bit more. My designs are starting to get repetitive, which usually means I have a lot more I want to do, but I haven't figured out how to make it work." She reached over and ran her hand from his head down his back, igniting his happy little purr. "But the best thing about creativity is that it spawns **more** creativity." She laughed and got up, heading to their coat rack, a new edition to their room.

*So designing things for this idea gave you ideas for other things?* he asked. He wasn't creative like she was, had never felt a spark of inspiration the way she did. It seemed important to understand the way his witch looked at things.

"Effectively, yeah," she agreed. "Only this idea was for something I've already made. An improvement on a past idea." She pulled her butterfly capelet off the rack, holding it out as though displaying the wings.

*Why would you change that?* he asked. *It's purrfect.*

As he'd hoped, his compliment made her smile wider, a little pink brightening her cheeks. "You're so sweet, Kitty."

He liked the capelet. She'd been designing it when she first brought him home, and he'd been with her when she bought the fabric. It was the first of many things she'd made to accommodate his claws and preference for her shoulder as a perch.

She brought the capelet back over to her desk. "I'm not going to change anything about the physical design. But I want to add something that I can trigger with my magic."

He stared at the capelet for a moment, wondering what it could possibly do if enhanced with magic. *I don't understand.* He shook his head, baffled.

"It doesn't need additional protection spells beyond what I've already sprayed on," Brigitte explained. "But something like that could be an option."

*You have something else in mind for it? Something other than a protection spell?* he asked. What other options were there? Camouflage, maybe? It **did** stand out.

She hesitated a moment. "Sometimes I think about the things that went wrong when I was fighting Celeste or that demon," she explained, her fingers tracing the black veins in the design. "But instead of dwelling on them, I try to think about how I would do things differently in the future."

*You plan a lot,* he said. *You're very good at it.*

She laughed. "You're not wrong. I think I almost always have backup plans, to the backup plans, to the plans." She lifted one side of the capelet and let go, watching it float back down. "Planning works well with my creation magic."

*Ruhul told me that once. It makes sense.* There was a lot about magic he didn't understand, and even with her good explanations, he didn't always get it.

"What if," she said slowly as she lifted the capelet up again. "I could use magic to make it into a shield?" It didn't feel like quite what she was looking for, and her magic merely flickered, rather than blossoming the way it usually did when she created something truly inspired.

It had started with the clothing spray she and Ruhul made to deflect harm. Embedded passive magic was easy to do, and it would hold up for many weeks once applied. They'd made enough for her parents, Ruhul, Aalia, Hēi Māo, and herself. Then her brain started coming up with other ideas. Ways to infuse designs or clothes with magic that could be triggered when needed.

Some of the ideas were such a big stretch for her, that it took several attempts to design something that looked like it would actually work. This was definitely going to be part of her *première* progressive. It was going to help her, had already helped her grow as both a designer and magic user.

She would have liked to test some enhancements on Hēi Māo's clothes, but they still didn't have a strong handle on his magic. If he couldn't trigger it, the enhancement wouldn't do him any good.

She looked over to her familiar, in his black cat form, sprawled in the sunbeam on their floor. It was good to see him so relaxed again. The first few days after the vandalism, he'd been tense and morose. Then he came home from an appointment with Dr.

Wheeler, their therapist, and asked for a family meeting. He shared that he felt responsible for the damage. He was afraid they'd get hurt and it would be his fault. When he looked at it rationally, he knew it wasn't his fault, but emotions didn't listen to logic. There had been a lot of hugs and some discussion about how they could stay safer going forward.

They were about halfway through winter break now. There had been no other attacks on Nikli. Or any that had been attempted had been utterly thwarted by the powerful protection spells and enchantments she and her parents had placed on the building and the sidewalk once the repairs were done. It had been so nice to be away from the pettiness they'd been facing at school. They'd had a movie night and a game night with Aalia and Ruhul. Aalia's website had really taken off once the construction crew shared it with their friends and family. While their friend wanted an audience that included non-shape-shifters who were open to changing their perspective, having a large shifter following would encourage her to handle sensitive information properly. It also meant she had an audience she could go to for fact checking and additional story ideas. She'd found two writers in the shape-shifter community who wanted to regularly provide articles for her, and the first of those had already gone live with great response.

Brigitte added a few more design ideas to her sketchbook. None of these were quite what she wanted. They felt like they were transitions between the nebulous initial idea and something new and truly ground-breaking. She was on the right track, and just needed a little more time, or maybe a nudge in the right direction.

Under a pile of fabric on her desk, her phone suddenly let out a ringtone she never liked hearing. She frantically dug out the device, swiping to answer. "Hello?" She swiveled in her chair to check on Hēi Māo. Anything related to his father tended to make him tense.

"Good day, Mademoiselle Defresne-Li," he drawled. "Given the current state of public opinion, we need to have a discussion."

The fact that **he** was calling her himself, rather than having his assistant do it, provided an extra serving of ominous to what she already felt. "I understand." Was he going to wash his hands of them now that the backlash had started? While she detested the man, Hēi Māo genuinely enjoyed working for him now that he had control over his schedule and volume of jobs. She couldn't deny that she'd loved the exposure and the experience of working backstage during a show. "Did you want to talk now, or..."

He stepped in to finish the thought for her. "I think it would be best to have this conversation in person."

"Okay," she agreed. "We're on winter break until March eleventh, so we're pretty flexible."

"Will tomorrow at three fit your schedule?" he asked.

She remembered Hēi Māo's advice from before the first meeting they'd ever had with Pierre Parenteau. She couldn't let him think he had all the control. "Two-thirty would be better," she offered. "We could meet at that cafe across from Parenteau headquarters. Lucky Bug."

"I'm not sure such a public setting suits our needs," he said, his voice as cold and unaffected as usual.

"They have a small meeting room at the back," she pointed out. "It has a door we can close, and no outside windows."

"Hmmm. I suppose if a space of that nature is available, it would suffice," he allowed.

"I'll contact them right now and make arrangements," Brigitte offered. "I'll send you a confirmation once I know if it will work."

"Very good." She could practically see his sharp nod. "I look forward to seeing the both of you tomorrow at two-thirty, at the Lucky Bug Cafe. Good day." The phone went silent and the call dropped.

# *Chapter Nine*

Brigitte made her way up the stairs from the subway. They were in one of the more modern parts of Paris, with taller buildings, standardized cement sidewalks, and more traffic of all kinds. Her arm was tucked into the sling where Hēi Māo lay. He'd been so anxious about this meeting, reminding her of the first time they'd met his father. She'd considered having one of her parents come with them, to help him feel more secure, but decided against it. She'd gotten pretty good at handling Pierre Parenteau herself, and she would have no qualms about leaving in the middle of their meeting if things weren't going well. She also suspected he'd take offense at her including anyone he hadn't specifically invited, simply to make things more difficult.

She continued to run her hand over Hēi Māo's side, occasionally brushing under his chin in an effort to soothe him. She could feel the steady vibration of his anxious purr against her abdomen. She wondered if he needed to take something for his anxiety, but it wasn't a constant thing. In fact, it was highly predictable. Seeing his father outside of modeling work was the greatest trigger.

*Are you going to be okay?* she asked. He barely ate breakfast and hadn't even touched his lunch. Then he'd meekly asked to travel to the meeting as a cat, something he usually just did, no permission required.

*Yeah.* Under her fingers, she felt him take a deep breath.

*You're catastrophizing, aren't you.*

He went utterly still for a moment. *No?* There was a pause. *Maybe?*

She scratched around his ears. *We'll be okay,* she promised.

*What if he doesn't want me to model anymore?* he asked, his mental voice painfully meek.

*You don't need the money.*

He let out a huff. *That's our capital for launching Butterfly fashions.*

It hadn't occurred to her that losing the arrangement with Pierre would do more than hurt her visibility. *It's **your** savings, to do with what you want,* she insisted.

He squirmed, then crawled out of the sling. Though the sidewalk wasn't crowded, he dashed to the nearest alley. He came out in his human form. She'd found that he didn't mind shifting in front of their family or close friends, but it wasn't something he wanted just anyone to see.

He took her hand, tugging her out of the flow of passersby. He tilted his head to look at her from under his tousled bangs. It was totally unfair when he used his modeling and good looks against her like that. "I need you to listen for a moment. This is really important to me."

She nodded, unable to make her throat work.

"I know you don't own me any more than I own you. That we're a partnership." He shook his hair out of his face, all the better to pin her down with his intense gaze. "I never **dared** to have dreams for my future before I found you. You opened all the doors in the world for me. You showed me what it meant to have a passion, and you've shared that spark with me." He squeezed her fingers gently.

"You deserve your own dreams," she said, her voice a little rough. She couldn't imagine not having that freedom. She loathed his father, and once in a while Hēi Māo revealed something else she hadn't consciously known that made her want to arrange a meeting with Pierre is some dark alley. "You don't have to match mine."

He gave her a heart-stoppingly beautiful smile. "I know. But the miracle in all of this is that I really enjoy the business side of things. I **want** to do this with you. I want to be the one who gets to see how excited you are when something comes together. I want the skills to support your passion."

She reached up to rub behind his left ear, something they'd found that calmed them both. "You're a people pleaser, and I worry that you'll become the business side of Butterfly, and you'll hate it. That you'll resent me for trapping you there, the way your father trapped you in the past."

Hēi Māo shook his head. "I actually talked to Dr. Wheeler about this, you know."

That was a surprise. "No. I didn't."

He shrugged. "We talked about my past motives, discussing whether they'd been skewed by survival or selfishness."

"You're **not** selfish," she grumbled. No one could call him that.

"We all are sometimes," he corrected. "And that's okay. We just need to be aware of it and make sure we follow healthy patterns."

She nodded. Dr. Wheeler had been huge on communication and healthy patterns of behavior during her own sessions.

"How did you know fashion, design was your **thing**?" he

asked quietly.

That was a ridiculously hard question. "I... just did. It felt right with my magic and I... I loved it the moment I found it and understood it. I couldn't imagine not doing it."

"It's a really personal thing, right?" he asked.

She nodded again.

"I didn't leap to the idea of managing your business on a whim," he explained. "It came together slowly. I liked the business class last semester. I understood when you told me about the costs and qualities of fabrics and other supplies. I knew it was what I wanted before I showed you what I was."

She let out a sigh. "Okay. I... I can't argue with that. And I'm going to believe you when you say it's what you really want." She still had to make sure he had an out though. "But I need you to understand that you're allowed to change your mind if you find something else that you enjoy later. If you want to try other things."

"Thank you," he said. "I don't think that'll happen, but I'm glad to know it's an option. He looked around and gave her hand a tug before letting go. "We should get moving."

Hēi Māo sat beside his witch, his hands wrapped around his mug of chai. He sniffed the steam, trying to let the cinnamon and cardamom soothe him. The Lucky Bug Cafe's private meeting room was bright and cheerful, making up for its lack of windows with murals of impressionist gardens, populated by ladybugs and butterflies. If it weren't so close to the Parenteau headquarters, he'd love to come back here some time when he didn't feel like he was going to throw up.

He'd tried tuning out his father as he settled in at the long table across from them, but that made Hēi Māo feel guilty. He couldn't make Brigitte face his father alone.

"Good afternoon Mademoiselle Defresne-Li." His father nodded before focusing his blue eyes on Hēi Māo. "Tom," he said grudgingly. It might have been the first time Pierre had used his new name without needing to be reminded.

"Good afternoon Monsieur Parenteau." Brigitte gave him a professional smile, very surface with no hint of her emotions bleeding through. Hēi Māo was impressed by how well she was masking her true feelings. "What did you wish to discuss with us?"

"Our arrangement may well have reached an end," his father said. His posture grew more stiff and defensive, which didn't seem possible. "While it seemed advantageous for both of us initially, public opinion is fickle and we are beginning to see a negative impact from Parenteau marketing featuring... Tom."

His father had changed very little. He still openly discussed his son as though he wasn't there. Once it would have bothered him, back when he still eagerly sought his father's approval and affection. Now, he was just as happy to not have that focus directed on him. He had a new family, and they were effusive in their love.

Brigitte nodded. "That seems to follow along with the backlash we've encountered in recent weeks."

"I can not risk subjecting Parenteau to this controversy further," Pierre continued. "I've already pulled the ads and images the marketing department identified as the most problematic, and I can't imagine that I'll be able to use Tom in future campaigns, possibly ever."

*I'm sure dear old dad is devastated,* Brigitte told him. Despite no change in her outward expression, her sarcasm came through their minds just fine. *But probably all the better for you.* With a faint smile, she folded her hands on the table and made his father meet her eyes. "I understand." How was she able to look directly into his father's face and not recoil? "I'm not entirely surprised." His father must have communicated something with his expression, because she continued as though he'd spoken. "This isn't an issue you truly feel strongly about," she explained, almost dismissive. "We used your support to keep the less pleasant truths concealed, and it's no longer convenient for you to maintain that illusion."

"It leaves me back where I was when we first negotiated," he pointed out. "Short a trained model capable of providing the breadth needed at Parenteau."

His witch shrugged. "It's hardly my fault if you've chosen to cut him from your lineup."

"It was your idea to go public," he countered.

Hēi Māo scowled. *I think he's trying to suggest you're the one who broke the contract, not him. Not sure why he cares. Probably just wants power over you... or me.*

*Or us.* Brigitte tilted her head. "You would have preferred a scandal, then? Because people would have figured it out. It wouldn't have taken long once I started showing up at school with Tom Hēi, formerly Jacque Parenteau, instead of my familiar."

Hēi Māo thought she was giving people too much credit. But it only took one wrong person to discover a secret before it became a tabloid best seller.

"I'm not sure how you want me to fix this for you," Brigitte went on. "If you choose to break our agreement, that's fine. We'll go our separate ways, content that we've done what we could to aid in your adjustment to the changes."

"I'm not **choosing** to break our agreement," Pierre growled. "I'm making a sound business decision. But I can't expect you to understand that." That last bit came out dismissive enough that Hēi Māo felt he ought to intercede in her honor. He only held back because he suspected that she'd be irritated if he leaped onto the table in between them to hiss at his father. She didn't generally mind cat behavior in his human form, but he'd probably just spill her tea and make Pierre even more difficult to work with.

Brigitte sniffed and rolled her eyes just enough to send a message without being obnoxious. "I've grown up helping my parents run a business, and I've started my own. I think I understand sound business practices just fine." She leveled his father with a glare. "You knew shape-shifters were controversial when you agreed to the plan, but I understand if it's more than your company can weather." She smirked a little, her bright blue eyes flashing. "But don't blame me when the people of Paris eat you alive for turning your back on your son at the first sign of trouble."

Pierre stared at her, clearly stunned.

"Tom Hēi's fan clubs have been growing, you know." Brigitte shrugged. "I expect they'll be quite put out when he stops appearing in your shows and ads. You'll need a good cover story to convince them you didn't ditch your son and the memory of your beloved wife simply because haters were nibbling at your bottom line."

Hēi Māo stared at her in awe. Everything about her read as casual disinterest, and she'd pointed out something he hadn't even considered. Public pressure could go more than one way.

Pierre leaned back in the hard-backed wooden chair. "And I suppose you have a good cover story for this."

"Me?" Brigitte said as if surprised. "Goodness, no. I'm a designer, not a writer."

There were several minutes of uncomfortable silence at the table.

"I think," Brigitte slowly said, finally cutting into the tension. "If you want to keep his fans off your back, you probably need to give the whole shape-shifter support thing a more solid try before you give it up."

Hēi Māo couldn't stop the smile creeping over his face when he felt the first spark of her creation magic. It was a subtle warmth, slowly growing, like being close to one of his Brigitte's candles.

"What kind of nonsense is that?" Pierre demanded.

Brigitte shrugged. "You made one announcement back in November in support of your son, but you've not done anything else to suggest that you really care about the bigotry his people face."

"Do you expect me to make a donation to charity, Mademoiselle Defresne-Li?" he asked sourly. "Publicly announcing my support for your cause?"

"That would hardly be helpful," Brigitte said with a snort. "Though I suppose you could go with chastising the general population. I don't think I've ever met someone with such high-level shaming skills as you."

Hēi Māo bit his lip to avoid laughing at her joke. Pierre stared at her in confusion.

Brigitte sighed. "That's very short term, too. What you really need is to do something more in line with Parenteau's mission…"

Hēi Māo felt her excitement bubbling up as the idea fully blossomed in her mind. For small things, modifications of designs or quick creations, the magic felt warm and vibrant. This time it was much stronger. He wondered if he could actually see the brightness coming off her, or if that was his imagination.

"Such as?" Pierre prompted, clearly not aware of the inspiration taking place across the table.

Hēi Māo reached down to her backpack and pulled out her sketchbook, sliding it to the table in front of her. Then he carefully tucked the pencil into her seeking hand.

She mumbled something completely unclear and turned to a blank page.

When Pierre opened his mouth to speak, probably to demand an explanation, Hēi Māo held up one hand to him. "A moment, sir. We don't interrupt creation."

Brigitte's pencil flew across the page, capturing preliminary designs. He could clearly see the book while sitting beside her, and Hēi Māo realized she hadn't gotten just one idea. She was blocking out an entire line. Three on a page, hasty notes scrawled down the right margin, indicating fabrics, colors, and embellishments if she was staying true to her pattern. She flipped the page and continued with the next three.

He glanced up at Pierre, grinning at the sheer awe he saw there. His witch had surprised him with this flurry of activity. She'd gotten through four or five pages when she suddenly stopped and stared at the designs under her fingers silently. Over the course of ten minutes, she'd created an entire collection, each design distinctly different from the others. He couldn't see her notes clearly enough to identify the theme, but he could feel that she'd gotten down the basics, which meant her next step would be refinement.

"What under the stars was that?" Pierre asked, his voice hushed in a way Hēi Māo was certain he'd never heard the man speak.

"Raw inspiration," Hēi Māo replied. He leaned over to glance at her mug. It was empty, so he pushed his own into her hands. "You should drink this, my Gitte," he said. "Do you need anything else?"

Brigitte shook her head, still looking a little dazed.

"A scone maybe?" he offered.

"Not yet," she said.

Hēi Māo turned back to Pierre. "You'll need to excuse us for that interruption. I think that one was a long time in the making. She's been pushing at an idea for a week and a half."

Brigitte nodded in agreement.

"That's something that regularly happens?" Pierre asked.

Brigitte shrugged.

"It's not like weekly or anything," Hēi Māo said. "And most of the time it's an idea here and two there, that kind of thing. It's not usually an entire line at once."

"Is it possession?"

"Possession?" Hēi Māo repeated in surprise. That possibility hadn't occurred to him.

"No," Brigitte said softly. "It's like Hēi Māo said, raw inspiration. It's not normally that strong or that... much." She flipped through the pages and shook her head. "Where were we?"

"You were talking about how Parenteau could show support for shape-shifters by remaining true to its mission," Hēi Māo prompted. "But I'm not sure what you meant by that."

Brigitte nodded. She was starting to look a little less fuzzy and befuddled. "The Parenteau mission is to elevate people with innovative designs that allow them to express their personality while making a statement," she said dramatically.

Hēi Māo was impressed; he didn't think he could recite the company mission. Actually, he **knew** he couldn't.

"It's pretty easy to combine that with the concept of promoting change and influencing people through art," Brigitte said, shrugging as if it were no big deal.

Pierre folded his hands on the table. "Please go on," he encouraged.

"I have an idea for a collection that focuses on variability and change," Brigitte said. "This is something we want in our clothing, in our entertainment, in our lives. We shouldn't be afraid of change in our friends and neighbors." She grinned at Hēi Māo.

Pierre let out a huff. "Would this include the designs you just sketched out?"

"Some of them, anyway." Brigitte nodded. "I've been trying to do something in this direction for weeks, and it just finally came together."

"Have you ever provided a proposal pitch, Mademoiselle?" Pierre asked.

She nodded. "We have to do them in school for our progressive projects and I've done smaller scale versions for my clients."

"Would you be able to provide a pitch with samples in… say one week's time?" he asked.

Hēi Māo frowned. *That's not reasonable.*

Brigitte paged through her designs. "There's no way I could have the entire collection fabricated that quickly. But I could pitch a sample of… say the three outfits complete with the rest in technical design form with fabrication to follow soon after I have your feedback."

Pierre took a deep breath, looking them both over for a moment. "Very well. I shall select an appropriate meeting space for this time next week, and you may pitch your shape-shifter collection to me then. If I like it," he paused. "**If** I like it, Parenteau will back your collection's debut and initial production. This will show my support for my son and his future well-being without putting the Parenteau brand at further risk."

"That's a brilliant plan, Monsieur Parenteau," Brigitte agreed.

*I feel like there's a catch somewhere,* Hēi Māo cautioned, though he couldn't imagine what it was.

*Probably. But designing an entire line by next week is happening whether he partners with us or not,* she replied. *These are just the preliminary ideas.* She patted her sketch book. *There's many more where these came from.*

Pierre stood, nodded to them both and left the room.

"Well that… definitely could have gone worse," she said, giggling nervously now that the scary parts were over.

"Can I get you that scone now? Maybe some more tea?" Hēi Māo asked.

"Only if you get something for yourself," she countered. "I'm sure you must be hungry by now."

He was about to deny it, but his stomach's growl cut him off. "Yeah. You stay here. I'll order up snacks."

## *Chapter Ten*

Their room was an unmitigated disaster. There were patterns draped over chairs, half-completed outfits and accessories folded in haphazard heaps over his bed, and other pieces in more complete stages hanging from his privacy curtain rod.

They were halfway to the one-week deadline Pierre had given her, and Hēi Māo wasn't entirely sure from moment to moment if Gitte could possibly succeed. She was going to need the last week of winter break to recover, either way.

She'd used nearly all her profit from the last four months of commissions to buy the fabric for the first six outfits she had planned. She'd explained that she planned to make the entire collection whether or not Parenteau backed it, because it was exactly what Paris needed right now. A reminder that change and variety were good, while also allowing the comfort of something not too far out of the ordinary.

He loved her dedication, but wondered how she would accomplish it on her own. Finding solid investors and business partners was hard.

"Please try to stay still," Brigitte begged, sounding exasperated as she knelt beside Aalia to adjust the hem. "This is a critical point. If I fuck this up, the dynamic element won't work right, and it'll just look sloppy."

"So sorry, girl," Aalia said, cringing in embarrassment. "I'm just so excited."

"Chill, Aalia. It's not like this is your first Gitte… or Butterfly original," Ruhul called out from behind the privacy screen where he was getting dressed.

"Yeah, but this is a whole ensemble," Aalia insisted, stopping herself from turning toward him without needing Brigitte to call her out again. "It's designed for me." She thumped her chest. "My body type and size, and I'm getting to model it for a pitch." She squealed a little.

"And hopefully for the show," Brigitte added.

"No way he'll go for that," Aalia scoffed. "Crabby old man favors skinny little stick people." Genetics had graced her with generous curves, and they suited her.

"You're not wrong about that," Hēi Māo agreed with a frown. His diet had been so carefully controlled that it had apparently stunted his growth and muscle development, both of which could have hurt his modeling career and health. Moving in with the Defresne-Li family righted that balance, resulting in a couple of excruciating growth spurts over the winter.

"Butterfly prefers **real** people," Brigitte said with a sniff. "I'll not be designing exclusively for one body type. That's terribly short-sighted. Most of the population can't wear Parenteau because it's so limited in who it really flatters."

"Pierre believes true fashion belongs to the elite, that it **should** be limited," Hēi Māo said. He'd heard enough comments during shows and shoots, where his father – gods it felt weird to call him that – cut models who didn't fit the image, or who had 'gained a bit

71

too much chub,' since their last appearance with him. Shaming people over their weight was huge backstage.

Brigitte looked up at Aalia, reaching out to pat her wrist. "You and I should never wear the same style of anything, because what you rock makes me look scrawny. And what suits me best would be all tight in weird places on you."

"Can't argue with that," Aalia agreed.

Ruhul let out a bark of laughter, and the rest of them all turned toward the screen.

"You have to share," Aalia said. "You can't laugh like that and not share."

"I'm just..." He took a deep breath, possibly to quell the chuckles. "I'm trying to imagine Gitte in your clothes, and... she'd look like a kid who'd raided her big sister's wardrobe."

Brigitte snorted. "Honestly, I think it's to my advantage to pitch a clothing line that has a different appeal." She leaned back to look at Aalia. "Slow spin please?" She watched, nodding, before continuing her thought. "Pierre's been featuring my work because he has to if he wants to keep Hēi Māo as a model. He almost always chooses one of my designs that aims for a slightly different clientele than his own collection at the time. Not enough to reflect badly, but enough to stand out as other."

"The stuff I've modeled for Gitte makes Butterfly look like rival fashion house," Hēi Māo explained when Aalia looked puzzled. "This –" He pointed to Aalia's outfit. "Makes it look like Butterfly is no longer a threat to him. She isn't going after **his** customer base. She's going after a base he doesn't even want."

Brigitte beamed up at him. "You really do have a mind for the business side of this, don't you."

It made him feel all warm and happy when she was pleased with him. Almost as nice as lying in a sunbeam.

"Change out of that, Aalia," Brigitte said. "I need about fifteen more minutes on it, then we can test the dynamic function."

Ruhul stepped out from behind the changing screen, looking a little stiff in his outfit. "I'm trusting you here, Gitte, but I'm not sure this one's my style. It's comfortable, but... I think it's a bit too big."

Hēi Māo looked at their friend, seeing what he meant. "She went a little long and wide on that on purpose," he explained, helping settle the shirt where it needed to be for the fitting. "It's much easier to remove fabric than add it."

"How do you add fabric?" Ruhul asked.

"By starting over," Hēi Māo replied, delighted when his quip made them all laugh.

"Sometimes you can rip it apart and replace a panel with something bigger," Brigitte added. "But it depends on the design and the fabric. Not all materials are forgiving."

While Brigitte started adjusting Ruhul's shirt, Hēi Māo went to the wall of crates they'd set up beside the open trapdoor leading to the family apartment. She'd needed so many new and different materials for this collection, and they needed a place to store everything so they could actually put things together. Some of the crates were nearly empty, a good sign as those were materials for the outfits in the most complete state. Others were full, for the designs she hadn't started yet. He refolded some fabrics and put them back where they belonged.

He'd learned to pin patterns, but there was a definite limit to what he could do for his witch during the actual creation of clothes. As he did when she was designing, he looked for the things he could do to support what she was working on. Keeping her work space as safe and tidy as possible had become his primary focus during this big project.

"Do you see it now?" Brigitte asked, excitement in her voice.

"Holy shit, Gitte," Ruhul gasped. "That's amazing!"

"Still think it's not you?" she teased.

Juniper let out a sassy string of yips from atop Brigitte's bed. "You know you love it."

Hēi Māo found himself laughing along with Ruhul.

"Thank you Juniper," Brigitte said, throwing a smile up to the fox. "Not sure what you said, but I know it was perfect."

## *Chapter Eleven*

Standing in the elevator, Brigitte stretched the sore muscles in her hands and upper back. Hunching over her patterns and the sewing machine for so many concentrated hours wasn't something she'd want to repeat too soon.

Pierre's assistant Madeline, a short woman who wore a sharp suit and a severe bun, stood directly in front of the doors. She'd spoken very little beyond greeting them and hadn't moved since pressing the floor button.

"Oh," Hēi Māo said softly. "I know where we're going." He waved one hand at the panel showing just one button near the top lit.

"I suppose you were here a lot in the past," Ruhul said. "I kinda forget that you're a world famous model sometimes."

"That's cool with me," Hēi Māo said, leaning over for a fist-bump.

"So where **are** we going?" Brigitte asked. "I've never set foot inside Parenteau before."

"There's a mini runway in one of the meeting rooms on the

twenty-eighth floor. Great view," he mentioned, offhand. "It's actually the best possible place for you to pitch your collection, because it really will give an accurate view of what you've done and how it will appear on stage."

"Does that matter?" Aalia asked, her hand wrapped tightly around the upright bar on Brigitte's mobile clothing rack.

Hēi Māo nodded. "Have you ever tried something on that looked really... meh on the rack, but was completely different once it was on a person?"

"Oh gods yes," Aalia said, nodding emphatically. "Point taken."

"My father is going to be looking at how these present almost as much as the actual design work," Hēi Māo explained. "Because that first look will determine if the item will catch enough customer attention to sell well."

"It's a gigantic numbers game," Brigitte said. "Sometimes designers will make something more for shock value or stretching the limits of fashion and art than practicality. Bespoke pieces and haute couture aren't intended to sell to the general population, or at all, in many cases." It was a side of fashion she'd decided early on that she had no interest in. Sure, she liked taking chances on things that stretched her abilities and imagination, but there was more than one way to do that. First and foremost, she wanted people to love the clothes they were wearing. The prêt-à-porter side of fashion, where she could produce ready-to-wear lines, was much more her style.

Her stomach dropped when the elevator stopped, but she suspected it had little to do with the movement. The doors slid open. She wasn't sure she'd ever been so nervous in her life. When she'd first met Pierre Parenteau, she'd been afraid, but it was more along the lines of what she felt facing the demon, fear for herself and her familiar. But this was different.

The success of this pitch had farther reaching potential

consequences than any of her other design efforts, ever. Her individual outfits at his shows had boosted her small business enough that she was getting regular work, but not so much that she couldn't keep up with school. Releasing a full collection, with the publicity a famous house could bring, was truly a once-in-a-lifetime chance. Most fully trained designers never had such an opportunity. It could launch Butterfly off Etsy and referral. She could potentially have a functioning design house with actual employees before she started university in another year. Of course, if this went wrong, it would hurt all the more, so she tried to remind herself that she had plans for success that didn't rely on this.

She followed Madeline out of the elevator. Hēi Māo and their friends trailed after with the carefully bagged outfits on the rack. Madeline led them to a long room, the bulk of which was taken up by a stark white runway with a black curtained stage. A small collection of chairs sat at the end, perfectly placed for evaluation.

"There is space for changing, as requested," Madeline said, gesturing to the matching curtained spaces off to each side of the stage. "Please get set up. Monsieur Parenteau will be with you in thirty-five minutes."

"Thanks, Madeline," Hēi Māo said. "I'll show them the ropes."

She looked at him for a moment, a small smile gracing her face. "It's wonderful to see you again, Tom." She turned and strode out of the room, her heels clicking against the floor tiles.

"Oh my gods," Brigitte whispered. "I feel completely out of my element." Everything in the room whispered of wealth and excess. The chairs were leather and brass. She was sure the view was amazing, but she barely glanced at it. She was excited to take charge of a real catwalk, something she hadn't been able to do as a guest designer at Pierre's shows. But maybe she **had** overstepped her abilities this time. Maybe she was about to flop spectacularly. She didn't really belong here. She shouldn't be trying to work with

Pierre Parenteau, the man who'd abused her kitty.

She heard the shuffling of hangers, realizing they didn't have a lot of time. They needed to be ready before Pierre showed up. This only made it harder for her to focus on what she needed to do. Hēi Māo handed garment bags to Ruhul and Aalia to take to the changing spaces. Brigitte hurried to take off her coat, hanging it on the rack just inside the door, where the others had already put theirs.

"Go ahead and put on your outfits," Hēi Māo said. "I'll help my Gitte with something else first. If we're lucky, we'll have a chance to do a practice walk before showtime." He looked happy. How was he happy to be here?

"Nervous?" he asked, reaching out to pull her close. "That's normal. Every designer who has ever entered this room has been nervous about it. Even the ones who actually work here and regularly collaborate with Pierre."

She'd noticed he'd become really selective about referring to the man as his father. She wondered if it was intentional. "I'm glad you're here with me," she said, her voice soft.

"Me too," he said. "It's so nice to see you getting the chance you deserve."

She snorted and shook her head.

"Come check this out," he suggested, leading her up onto the runway and then down the other side to reach the wall lined with large windows. "Close your eyes for me, Gitte."

His hands settled on her shoulders, and she realized all of a sudden how much larger they were than her own. Of course they'd grown along with the rest of him.

"Take a moment to just breathe," he murmured, his head near hers so he could speak into her ear. "In… and out… and in… and out."

She followed his instruction.

"Now take a moment to focus on what you can hear," he suggested.

The soft shuffling noises of Ruhul and Aalia getting dressed. The fans in the ceiling.

"Now I want you to open your eyes," he said.

The view of Paris from twenty-eight floors up **was** breathtaking. The Seine sparkled, reflecting the mid-afternoon sunlight. She reached out to touch the glass, then thought better of it. She didn't dare leave smudges.

*Better?* he asked.

*Better,* she agreed. She took one last deep breath and turned to him with a smile. "You go get dressed. I'm going to set up the design lookbook." She pulled the binder off the rack and carried it to the end of the runway, where she was quite certain Pierre would sit. She would have preferred to have it more artistically bound, but she simply hadn't had the time. The lookbook contained a fifteen-outfit collection, not just the four designs she'd managed to complete. She glanced through the pages one last time, hoping she wouldn't find any horrible problems at this point. As she resolutely closed the cover, Aalia came out from behind the curtain to stand on the runway.

"C'mon, Gitte. Shouldn't you be getting changed too?" Aalia asked, then she sauntered down the catwalk, striking three poses at the end. Then she dramatically tugged at the laces concealed at the waist to swiftly convert her curve hugging maxi-skirt into a delightful ruched mini.

"When did you practice all that?" Brigitte asked, stunned by her friend's skills. "I thought you said you'd never modeled before."

Aalia flashed her a radiant smile before converting the dress back to a maxi. "I've never modeled before. But I have this amazing friend who's like a **total** supermodel," she gushed. "And he's really good at teaching the whole thing." She flicked her fingers at the runway. "I'm feeling really good about representing you now."

Brigitte stepped back up onto the runway and hugged her friend. "You're amazing and I love you. Thank you for doing this."

"I'm glad to help." She gave Brigitte a gentle push. "Now go get changed. I think it would be nice if we could do a full walk through before Monsieur Parenteau gets here. I just **look** like I have nerves of steel."

"A walk-through would be really good," Brigitte agreed wistfully as she hurried into the curtained space. She'd only practiced in a taped space at home, and that was nothing like a real runway. Aalia's clothes were flopped over the small rack where her own outfit still hung, closed in it's bag. She pulled down the zip to remove the dress she'd made for herself. Aalia needed something that showcased her curves. She, on the other hand, wanted something a bit more classic that highlighted her arms and legs a bit. The red halter bubble dress was suitable for a party or special event.

She shucked her clothes, much the way Hēi Māo did for fittings and backstage quick changes, and suddenly understood that skill in a more concrete way. She threw them over the bar before slipping the dress off its hanger. Black beads dotted the bodice like stars in the night sky of an alternate universe. She tugged gently on the sides of her backless bra before fastening the halter behind her neck. She was focused in the moment, just herself with one of her greatest creations.

"Hey boys, how you doing over there?" Aalia called, her footsteps firm but not obnoxious as she continued to practice. "You're being awful quiet."

"That's because I'm trying to sit still for my makeup sesh," Ruhul called back. "There was no way I was trying this solo, and I do **not** want Cat-dude to mess up."

Juniper let out a series of yips that sounded like fox laughter.

"I bet you're hot with makeup on," Aalia said, and Brigitte smiled knowing the comment was totally serious.

"Cat-dude has mad skills," Ruhul replied. "You'll be begging him for tutorials after you see me."

"I'm not **that** good," Hēi Māo insisted. "You should see my usual stylist. He's wicked with eyeliner."

Brigitte smiled and shook her head while sliding her arm into a black over-the-elbow glove. "You're no slouch with the eyeliner, Kitty." He'd helped with her makeup before their friends arrived to ride over together.

"Gitte, you need me to do anything else out here, or back there?" Aalia asked.

"I'm nearly ready, and everything out there is done," Brigitte called through the light curtain.

"I'll just keep strutting my stuff, then," Aalia said. "And you let me know if there's anything I can do to help."

They ended up having time for two practice runs, once with the music Ruhul had mixed for them, by the time Pierre arrived. Brigitte stood behind the black curtain in the tiny, crowded backstage area with Aalia. Hēi Māo and Ruhul were across the stage in their own cramped space. Juniper scampered out of the boys' changing area to nudge Ruhul with her muzzle, before peeking under the curtain and scampering back to the changing space. Brigitte peered through the weave of the fabric to see Pierre stride over to the chairs at the end of the runway. He settled into his seat, her lookbook in his hand.

*You got this,* Hēi Māo assured her, grinning and giving her a cheerful thumbs up.

"You may begin when you are ready," Pierre announced, with the air of one conferring a great honor.

She nodded to Hēi Māo and he tapped at his phone. Since he was the only one who wasn't suffering from first-time modeling jitters, he was running the audio.

The sweet tinkling of wind chimes came out of the speakers. "Introducing Shift, by Butterfly." Ruhul had worked with effects to make his voice sound a little lower and smoother, like an actual announcer. "Because your clothes should be as dynamic and versatile as you."

Her music kicked in, thirty seconds of cheerful pop that she could use to dance-walk down the runway. Her skirt swished. She dipped her hands into the large pockets tucked below the black belt cinched at her waist. Directly in front of Pierre, she took the time for two poses, giving him a look at the front and back of the dress. Then she grabbed the wrap-around zippers at the top of the pockets, giving them a decisive tug to convert the skirt from a plain red mini bubble to a below-the-knee flare. The inverted skirt had an overlay of black polka-dotted mesh that came down in points, leaving a border of bold red at the bottom. As she spun to show off the flow of the skirt, she raised her hands, and pushed one thumb around her other wrist to release the magnet that attached the hand to the glove. With both hand pieces off, the gloves had become independent sleeves. She swept her arms about, then turned and dance-walked back down the runway.

The music switched, and it was Ruhul's turn. He'd also gotten lessons from Hēi Māo, utterly outstripping her expectations. Her long-time friend was a natural, and she wondered if he'd be willing to model for her regularly. He seemed to have fun showing off the adjustable width on his pant legs, the casual shirt that could convert into a longer tunic, and the removable sleeves. Aalia went next, with the slinky music Ruhul had chosen to fit her personality and outfit. She was downright sassy when she reached up to her shoulders and tugged down the sheer bell sleeves hidden in the sleeveless top.

Hēi Māo went last. They'd decided that finishing with the most polished presenter could only serve them well. Now that she'd taken a turn at it herself, she realized just how good he was. He made it look easy, when it was anything but. He just flowed down the catwalk, every move graceful and fluid. At the end, he struck a pose, tilting his chin up, before grinning and showing how his vest could easily become a v-neck shirt. He lounged on the stage and kicked a foot in the air. With some quick finger work, he unfastened some decorative buttons on the ankle and knee to open up the side of the pant leg to display an inverted pleat with a bold contrasting color. Then he was up and walking back.

When the final music kicked in, the four of them stepped out together. Hēi Māo caught Ruhul under one arm and Aalia under the other, while Brigitte stepped to the front.

When the music faded, she gestured to the lookbook in Pierre's hands. "I do have several more outfits planned that fit the season and theme." She couldn't tell if he was revolted or intrigued. The man had a face of stone.

He flipped through the designs she'd laid out, finally closing the book as he stood up. "You are going to take the fashion world by storm one day, Mademoiselle Defresne-Li. It would be an honor to back your project."

# Chapter Twelve

Winter break was over, and the next few weeks flew by. While there were still regular problems with some of the kids at school, it was somehow less upsetting. Brigitte wasn't sure if that was because they'd had a break from the daily hostility, or if it was due to their own big projects eating up all their time and energy.

*Miraculous Morph*'s following continued to grow. Aalia had gotten a big bump after her first interview with a shape-shifter went up. Sure she got some traffic from trolls, but they were the minority and easily handled. Her meetings with various shape-shifter groups had gotten her a number of useful contacts, and she'd picked up a couple excellent discussion and comment section moderators. She'd moved from two casual to three dedicated shape-shifter writers, ensuring new content on a daily basis.

"Your *première* progressive is turning out a lot bigger than I think you'd planned," Brigitte said, as they looked over the latest post. Her friend had teamed up with Madame Chien, the lawyer who'd moderated Brigitte's first meeting with Pierre Parenteau. In this post they'd discussed current laws that were designed to specifically target and disenfranchise shape-shifters. Brigitte hadn't been able to finish reading the first draft; it made her so angry she literally couldn't think straight. Now that it was published, she was trying to get through it in chunks because it was really important information.

"I mean," Brigitte continued. "This is so far above and beyond what's expected, the committee's going to need a whole rubric." She was sure to have one of the top picks for classes their final year.

"That seems to be going around," Aalia said with a laugh. "And while this is serving that purpose, I've gotta tell you, now that I'm doing it, I don't need the excuse of a class assignment or expanding my portfolio as a reason to keep it up." She rubbed her hands together. "You **know** how much I love investigative journalism."

Brigitte grinned. She'd gotten to see her friend discover this branch after she'd already excelled at basic reporting and feature work. She personally thought features would be the most fun, finding the everyday stories everywhere. But Aalia took to research like the reintroduction of otters to the Loir River. She **lived** it.

"This whole thing is investigative, looking at every possible angle of the subject. And there are so. Many. Angles." She waved jazz-hands by her temples in her enthusiasm. "It hits all my writer happy buttons. Plus it's for a cause I'm a hundred percent behind, so I'm super invested here."

"I'm so glad it's working out like that for you," Brigitte said. She was grateful, but she'd initially worried her friend was taking on too much in a fight that she didn't have to get involved in. But Aalia didn't love her friends by halves.

"And did Rhu tell you his revised plan?" Aalia asked, wiggling happily in her seat. The boys had gone to the bathroom, safety in numbers and all, so he wasn't there to hold her back or fan the flames.

"I knew about his earlier plan," Brigitte said. "He was exploring different types of music to see how culture influenced the sounds. Has he changed it again?"

"I'm not going to spoil it," Aalia said, though resisting was obviously a struggle. "You have to ask. I've never seen that boy geek out more than when he outlined it for me."

"Well now I'm super curious." Brigitte shook her head. "I hope they get back before the bell. I may die from the anticipation if I have to wait until next break."

Brigitte met with Pierre once a week since he'd accepted her pitch. He personally went over the designs she'd chosen, helping her make technical changes that would ultimately improve the look, result in fewer wardrobe malfunctions as the garments aged, and cost less to produce. He made recommendations on pieces to cut or include in the line-up to ensure the kind of variety that was needed for the introduction of the project to be successful. Her goal was to keep the pieces in an affordable price range, without shorting on quality. His experience and help had been invaluable. It pained her to admit that she was learning a lot from him, but the truth was, he'd taught her more in the last three weeks than she'd leaned in the previous three months on her own.

Hēi Māo attended the meetings in his cat form, nestled in his sling or perched on her shoulder. He'd recommended the Lucky Bug cafe conference room, and Pierre agreed that it might be more comfortable for all of them. Hēi Māo avoided talking to his father, not even passing greetings along through her, and Pierre seemed content to ignore his son. His own familiar never attended the meetings; apparently, she never left his mansion.

Every moment that wasn't spent at school or on homework was taken up by bringing her now polished designs to life. Brigitte also brought Pierre her finished pieces to discuss modifications or minor adjustments. While she was terribly proud of the work she'd already done, the initial sample pieces had to be redone to fit the show's color standards, now that she had access to fabrics her usual store didn't even carry.

*He's never been that complimentary to me,* Hēi Māo pointed out as she walked back to the subway station, her familiar tucked into his sling. *He's nowhere near as effusive as Papa, but he almost acts like a father to you.*

The comment hit her like a punch to the solar plexus, and she froze mid-step, grasping the railing. She closed her eyes and swallowed hard, pressing her forehead against the cold tiles. Their initial arrangement with Pierre Parenteau made her uncomfortable, something she'd grown accustomed to but hadn't faded despite Hēi Māo's insistence that it was okay. He **wanted** to keep modeling; it was comfortable and routine for him. That he'd managed to get her something out of it, seemed a pretty big bonus to him. But was it really a bad idea?

*Brigitte?* He squirmed out of his sling to her shoulder. *What's wrong? Are you okay?*

She definitely wasn't okay. She felt like she could throw up. Pierre had tortured his son. A witch's familiar meant more than anything else, and Pierre had caused irreparable harm to her most important person. He was the last person on earth she should be working with.

She didn't even realize she was crying until Hēi Māo's thumbs were on her cheeks, drying away the tears. When had he shifted?

"Hey," he whispered. "What's wrong?"

"I... I... ngh." It was too hard to get the words out.

He sat down on the stairs, pulling her into his lap. The only saving grace was that the metro wasn't particularly busy at this time of day, so people coming and going were perfectly able to get past them. *Whatever it is, we'll figure it out. Right?*

*I need to cancel the project. I can't do this, not with **him**.* Telepathy was enormously handy when you couldn't otherwise talk.

"Shh, shh," he said quietly. "Where did this come from?"

*He's a horrible man,* she said. Her hands went to his wrists, gentle, touching without wrapping around them. *He abused you, hurt you, made you think you weren't worth anything.*

She felt him sigh. "Yeah," he agreed. "Those are all things he did."

She looked at him in surprise.

His smile was a little sad. "Dr. Wheeler has been trying to help me understand," he explained. "She says that abuse victims, especially kids, have a lot of trouble realizing and accepting that what's been done to them goes beyond a guardian merely being strict or mean." He shrugged. "It finally sank in at our last meeting, and I see it now. Pierre abused me. And in his case it wasn't just that he was ignorant of how to be a good parent. He didn't commit the unintentional mishaps of a poorly educated father, like it is for some people. There's probably no parent in Paris who would think it's actually okay to handcuff their kid. But that's effectively what he did. He was actively awful because he didn't like what I was."

"Is that why you call him by name now?" she asked.

"Emotional distancing," he explained. "Sometimes it's easier for me to really look at it and understand it clearly if I... remove my sense of self from my history."

"That... that doesn't sound good." She frowned.

"That's because I'm explaining it badly." He thought for a moment, his free hand scrubbing idly at his wild blond locks. "Jacque Parenteau and Hēi Māo are the same, right?"

She nodded.

"And Pierre and my father are the same person, too."

She nodded again.

"I like to think of my life as two separate eras," he explained. "I can talk and think about what Pierre did to Jacque more clearly than when I try to think about what **my father** did to **me**. I think of my past with him as **Jacque's** past. It's mine, but from one remove."

"Oh." She could see how it would be easier to be critical and clear-minded when thinking about something done to someone else. It was like having a built in perfect allegory.

"Dr. Wheeler thought it would help me to actually **see** how damaging my childhood was." He shrugged again. "I just have to make sure I don't try to divorce myself from my past. It's still mine, still part of how I became who I am. We can't escape our past."

"Especially not if you have a business arrangement with your abuser," she snapped. "You shouldn't ever have to see him, Kitty. He doesn't deserve to be in your life."

"Is that why you cried?" he asked. "You know it was my idea."

How could she answer that. She wasn't at all sure why she'd cried. "You said he's been nicer to me than he ever was to you."

"It's true," he admitted. "Though he's been loads nicer to me since I became your cat." He grinned. "I don't think I still need... validation from him. I'm not fishing for the praise he never gave me before."

"Isn't it hard to be working with him now?" she asked.

He shook his head. "I hardly have anything to do with him, so I'm not really working with him. I model his clothes, but it's always done through you. And with Shift, I'm working with you; I'm either modeling for you or I'm a cat. It's your thing, I'm just here to help you."

*But I'm working with him,* she said firmly. *Your witch is working with your abuser. How can that not hurt you?* That was the part that bothered her most.

He gave her a hug, rubbing his cheeks against hers, something he liked to do regardless of his form. "Actually, I'm glad you talked him into this. That you convinced him."

How did that make **any** sense?

"You've gotten him to risk his reputation and spend money on a project that is in support of the very thing he hated in me." He chuckled. "That was a brilliant move, and it's probably the best revenge ever."

"Oh." She hadn't really thought of it that way. In a warped way, she was helping him get back at Pierre.

"I want you to be successful, Brigitte. I want Butterfly to become the biggest best brand in Paris and the world, not just because it will frustrate Pierre, but because you deserve it." His light eyes were wide with enthusiasm. The early spring chill had made his cheeks pink. "You've given me so much. Freedom. Happiness. Life. You have no idea. You can't possibly. And I want to give back to you, if I can. I want you to be as happy as you've made me."

## *Chapter Thirteen*

Sitting in the makeup chair, Hēi Māo closed his eyes and focused on the energy around him. It was the first Wednesday of their spring break, and his Brigitte's show was going to blow Parenteau's latest out of the water; he could feel it. This entire thing was her creation, it was like a complex layering of her magic, and he suspected that not even a natural disaster could disrupt it. Whether the line's success would continue past today was the only uncertainty.

"I understand that you're pleased with all of this," Stefan said, tapping his chin with a makeup sponge. "But I need a neutral expression on that pretty face of yours, Tom."

Hēi Māo laughed at his friendly and flamboyant stylist. "Sorry, Stefan." He relaxed his face and listened to the usual preshow activity. He'd always enjoyed the energy building up to performing for an audience, letting it fill and recharge him. With so much of that energy infused with Brigitte's creation magic, this was sure to be his best show yet.

"I've never mentioned this before," Stefan said as he applied foundation with quick gentle strokes, "but I'm really glad you bailed on your father and struck out on your own. You seem so much happier than you used to."

That was a surprise. Jacque Parenteau had always tried to present as a professional, detached and calm, with no emotional baggage. He'd never thought anyone could see past the facade to his unhappiness. As Hēi Māo, he was free of those restrictions, and had started to really embrace it.

"Your witch is a good egg, Kid."

Hēi Māo grumbled at being called a kid.

Stefan chuckled. "I've been your stylist since you were still learning to tie your shoes, Tom. I'll still be calling you kid when you're twenty-five, maybe even thirty." He'd had no problem adopting the new name, and he was one of few staff members who were comfortable touching him now that he was a bound familiar. "Your witch is an amazing designer, even better than your old man." He whispered that last bit. "And I can see that she's doing this line, this show, for you. That's a huge thing, Kid." He snorted. "Some designers would consider this kind of move, career suicide. I mean, there's a reason Parenteau is backing this from a distance." He went quiet as he started in on contouring.

Stefan wasn't wrong. While Pierre had leveraged his connections to ensure Shift by Butterfly would have a huge introduction, the Parenteau name was understated in all the marketing, almost mentioned as an afterthought rather than a bold statement. The show was being held in Grand Palais, one of the larger venues, something unheard of for such a new design studio. Invitations had gone out to investors, buyers, reporters, and the elite in waves until every ticket had sold. They were months ahead of spring fashion week, but it was still a highly sought after location for shoots and off-season shows. Brigitte almost had a panic attack when she heard where it would be happening. It was a huge site, not one she felt ready for. His witch was confident in her abilities, but she wasn't used to skipping to the head of the line like this.

Pierre had used mystery and intrigue, telling as little as he could get away with in each of his announcements. People had grown accustomed to seeing Butterfly's designs at Parenteau shows, but it had been more than a decade since the fashion giant had backed a launch; usually Pierre's practice was to buy the designs or hire the designer if he liked their work so much.

The blush brush tickled Hēi Māo's cheeks.

"I, for one, hope Shift is a resounding success," Stefan continued, now that he didn't have to focus so closely on his work. "It's an innovative idea, so from a fashion stand-point, it's fucking brilliant." There was a clatter of plastic handles colliding. "And it's a good cause."

"Thanks," Hēi Māo said. He'd been humbled whenever they found shape-shifter support in places they didn't expect it.

"I admit, I didn't really see how we treated shifters until you came out, and I had to rethink a lot of things." He sighed. "I wish I'd been able to realize it earlier, before I probably did and said a whole lot of inappropriate and insensitive garbage." Light swabs dusted his eyebrows. "I apologize for being a big stupid bigot."

Lips were always last, so as long as he spoke without moving, Hēi Māo could talk now. "You were never that bad, Stefan," he insisted. It was stupid to hold people's ignorant pasts against them, especially if they were trying to improve.

"Kid, when I came out as bi, my parents disowned me and I lost a lot of friends. We were still viewed as conflicted and greedy back then. I was a punchline. I was often seen as sub-human. I **know** I could have been better, should have been better," he admitted. "Anyway, I'd love to see Butterfly get the success to go independent, and if things go right today, that could definitely happen." There were sounds as he shuffled at his table again. "Time to make those eyes shine. Bree-Bree had some very specific requests here, so stay extra still."

"Bree-Bree?" He couldn't help but ask.

"Everyone I care about gets a nickname, Kid."

Brigitte took a deep breath as the wind chimes poured out of the speakers. The audience went silent. This was it. Her first full collection was about to go on stage, and there was pretty much nothing else she could do to fix or adjust a thing at this point. Her designs had to wow the audience on their own merits.

Hēi Māo's hands settled on her shoulders, his warmth immediately comforting her. She wore her bubble dress, redone in a richer burgundy.

*Embrace it,* he coached.

*Trying to.* She was excited her clothes were getting the kind of audience she'd dreamed of. But it had all been so rushed, and she worried Pierre had set her up to fail.

*Your first show only happens once,* he reminded her.

She nodded. She didn't want the experience to fly past without really engaging in it. *Things could still go wrong.* She was a planner by nature; it was her job to consider all the contingencies.

He let out an almost silent laugh, well below the sound of the music and the introduction, redone and lengthened by Ruhul. *Close your eyes and find the touch of your magic here.*

She turned her head to glance at him in surprise. Stefan had outdone himself on her request. Green cat-eye with wings of crystal. It wasn't so obnoxious that it didn't fit with the clothes. She didn't want makeup or styling to take away from the designs.

He winked, so she closed her eyes and centered herself. A moment later, she opened her eyes, and gasped at the brilliance. Strands of golden magic, her magic spread out from her hands to everything. The clothes radiated with her power, filling the models with creation and good luck. *How?*

*The designs aren't your only creation here, my Gitte.* She'd noticed he added the possessive to her name when he wanted to remind her that she wasn't alone. *Your magic influenced Ruhul when he worked on the playlist while you sewed. Your magic touched the models when we worked with them on walk through. Your magic touched **everything** in this show.*

For the first time that they were aware of, Hēi Māo wouldn't be the only shape-shifter hitting the runway. Aalia had helped her make connections with experienced models and new faces who wanted to be part of this show. He'd coached them all, helping them find the performance that best worked for the outfit and their comfort level.

*You planned the clothes, the models, and the order. This show, is your creation. Your magic won't let it fail.*

She smiled, suddenly feeling calm. This **was** her creation. She trusted her friends and the models. Even if Pierre had ulterior motives, the show would go as she'd planned.

There was a smattering of applause mixed with soft vocal reactions spoken by several voices at one time as the first model stepped out from between the curtains. A few moments later there was a burst of approval as she hit the T at the end of the runway, showing off the dynamic aspect of her outfit. She posed, tossed her head and strutted back. As she was taking her place in the final presentation lineup, she caught Brigitte's eyes, throwing her two enthusiastic thumbs up. Brigitte returned the gesture, her worries entirely replaced with excitement.

It was hot back stage, and ridiculously busy. Brigitte was able to be fully in the moment now, and she was grateful for Hēi Māo's help. Still, the show passed incredibly quickly, even with her focused on it. In what seemed like no time, Hēi Māo was lining up for his walk. She moved up near the left mid-stage traveler curtain so she could watch without being seen. Once again, he owned the catwalk, his movements sassy and smooth. He usually had to be serious, even dismissive when modeling for Parenteau, but in addition to wanting models who more accurately reflected the population, Brigitte needed the models to look happy in her designs. She'd never bought into the disaffected look of high fashion.

There were cheers and howls of glee when he struck his first pose. Despite the controversy over his nature, Hēi Māo was still Paris' darling. The crowd was delighted to see him, and it was probably a surprise, even though he'd been clearly marked as Butterfly's primary model in the past. He hadn't appeared in any Parenteau marketing since before she started working on Shift. The audience response only grew when he shed his shirtsleeves and quickly converted his top into a vest.

Soon he was walking back, and the other models were joining him on stage in front of the curtains, all to the sound of cheers and applause. It was her turn.

She gently touched the mic clipped to her collar, making sure it was still there. Then she approached the line of models from the back, stepping out through the opening they made for her.

Holy crap. Seeing all the chairs filled, or mostly filled, was so different from their practice runs. The audience sparkled like diamonds as flash after flash went off, capturing the moment. Brigitte took a couple of steps forward and raised her arms. There were a few loud hoots, and the ruckus died down.

"I'm Brigitte Defresne-Li, founder of Butterfly fashions," she announced. "And this..." She gestured behind her with both hands. "Is Shift, a collection featuring dynamic designs that allow you to change your look and extend your wardrobe. Variety is the spice of life, and fashion-forward Parisians deserve variety in their wardrobes."

She beamed out at the audience, applauding exactly where she hoped they would. When it was quiet again, she continued. "I am incredibly grateful to Parenteau fashion house for backing this collection and giving me the opportunity to share it with all of you. Shift is dedicated to my familiar Hēi Māo and his mother Ysabeau Parenteau, who were my inspiration. After all, who's better at changing their look than a shape-shifter?" The applause for that was a bit less enthusiastic, but not entirely absent. "Buyers interested in carrying Shift in their stores can contact the Parenteau distribution office for details and arrangements. Questions about future Butterfly designs and plans, should be directed to Butterfly's official email."

She caught the crossover zipper pulls of her dress between her fingers and took two steps forward before swiftly converting her dress. A ripple of approval ran through the crowd. She spun twice, showing off the new lines of the same dress. "Thank you all for coming. I hope you enjoyed the show."

## *Chapter Fourteen*

Brigitte sat on the couch, sandwiched between Aalia and Hēi Māo. Ruhul was on the other side of Aalia. Maman and Papa were on the nearby loveseat with Callie sprawled across their laps. A shiver ran down her spine and she rubbed her hands together while they waited through a commercial break.

"You okay, Gitte?" Aalia asked, frowning in concern.

She shrugged. "Just a little nervous."

"The interview is already over," Ruhul pointed out. "Not much you can do about it now." He looked at her from over Aalia's head. "I thought you were happy with how it went."

"I was," Brigitte said reluctantly. "But... it's so hard to really know how well a closed interview is going at the time."

Aalia let out a grumble of annoyance. "And **some** journalists use shitty underhanded tricks in post, to warp your answers to fit some sensational plan they have in mind."

Brigitte felt like something heavy had landed in her stomach. She glanced at her parents in concern. "You don't think Nala would do that, do you?"

The tense look her parents exchanged did nothing to ease her mind.

Hēi Māo leaned against her, his loud human purr soothing her. "If she makes you look bad or twists your words, we'll **never** babysit her daughter again," he said. "And she'll be out of luck if she ever wants another interview."

"If she's smart, she won't take that risk," Aalia added. "Based on the postshow coverage, Butterfly is a rising star. You'll be newsworthy for years to come, and she isn't gonna want to mess with her connections."

"I'm not the only friend she'd lose as a consequence," Maman said firmly. "Tuesday mahjong nights would be utterly devastated."

Their comments should have made her feel better, but she continued to twist her hands in knots until Hēi Māo caught one.

"Pierre doesn't tolerate reporters who try to play him as a fool," he said quietly as he flattened her hand in his. "He's got all sorts of legal riders attached to all of his appearance and interview contracts." He shrugged. "It's bad for business if your founder and CEO looks like an idiot on national television." He rubbed his head against her shoulder. "If nothing else, being interviewed with him provides you a little extra protection from editors who would splice in different questions than the ones you've answered or who would dice up your responses into inaccurate soundbites."

"Well yay," she said, completely unenthusiastic. It was reassuring, but she didn't want to be grateful to that man again.

The news show started, and Brigitte watched with a mix of fear and fascination as Nala Freis introduced her guests. It was the first joint interview she'd done with Pierre in the wake of Shift's release. They had a press conference coming up tomorrow afternoon, and another interview with *Numéro* in a couple of days. While she'd expected to get some publicity from the show, she hadn't thought she'd be in such high demand. She'd even gotten emails from a couple agents inquiring on pricing for bespoke designs for their clients' future events. She knew it was a mistake to wish the publicity would die down, but she hadn't factored this level of success into her plan.

It was going to be a scramble and a struggle to keep up with homework, as they approached the end of their *première* year. When they returned from spring break, they'd only have about a month left of regular classes. Then they'd have a week for revision, preparing them for exams, Summer Solstice, then a week of exams followed by a week of presenting their *première* progressive projects.

*I was at the interview, Gitte,* Hēi Māo reminded her. He'd sat next to her on the couch in cat form through the whole thing, making a point to sit on the side away from Pierre. *You did great.*

She reached for his hand on one side and Aalia's on the other as the stage came into focus. It was weird and uncomfortable to see herself on the television screen. Her posture initially looked a bit awkward, but it improved over the course of the interview. She couldn't fault her responses. She'd let Pierre do more of the talking, partly so he could show his support for shape-shifters and because he was more experienced.

"When Mademoiselle Defrense-Li shared her idea for a dynamic line in honor of shape-shifters, it seemed a fitting tribute to my missing wife and our beautiful son," Pierre explained.

"How exactly does shape-shifting play into the designs?" Nala asked. "And why would you go this route?"

"All the clothes have a dynamic element," on-screen-Brigitte said. "This allows the wearer to easily change their look." She beamed at the camera. "As you know, my familiar is a shape-shifter and I've seen how controversial the topic is. But it doesn't need to be this way. Looking at fashion, we all like to change our look from time to time, right?"

Nala nodded encouragingly.

"Why is it so wrong for shape-shifters to do the same?" television Brigitte asked. "After all, they can only be human **or** their animal, whereas magic users can use all sorts of spells to change their appearance, and anyone can do the same with their clothes, accessories or makeup."

"Ugh," Brigitte said. "That was heavy-handed, wasn't it."

"It was fine, Cupcake," her father replied. "And it's accurate."

"It really is your message distilled to its simplest form," Aalia added. "Now shush. I'm looking for elements to emphasize in my *Miraculous Morph* posts."

"Really?" Hēi Māo asked.

"I want to be sure I'm staying on brand, as they say in marketing." Aalia's grin was mischievous. "But I'm also using slightly different language so our connection isn't obvious. Viewers will think there's multiple groups supporting shape-shifters, and it will help normalize things."

"You're wicked sneaky," Ruhul said.

Juniper let out a little hum that seemed to be an agreement.

## *Chapter Fifteen*

He expected returning to the routine of school after the postshow media junket would be a relief. There had never been much of a reaction among their classmates after his usual shows, so he assumed no one was really into fashion. A few girls would ask him for autographs in a giggly shy way. The kids who were friendly with him would ask him how it went. The ones who shifter phobic would crack snide comments if they could catch him without fans around him. Pretty simple.

He was utterly flummoxed by how much the atmosphere at L'Étoile du Nord had changed after three weeks away.

"Great job, Brigitte, Hēi Māo," a guy called from a passing cluster of friends.

*Who was that?* he asked, after being completely unable to identify them.

Brigitte let out a nervous giggle as she continued rummaging in their locker. *No clue. Some terminale guy. I think I met him on student council last year.* She glanced up at him. *I wonder if Aalia and Ruhul are getting the same treatment.*

They'd come separately this morning because he and Brigitte had some paperwork to drop off at the office for the few upcoming absences they were expecting. He pulled out his phone and sent a text to their group chat, wishing them a good morning. Brigitte's phone chimed.

"That's just me messaging the group," he told her, so she could finish what she was doing without worrying that it was something important.

A minute later both their phones chimed, so he swiped his thumb over the screen. "They've become extra popular, too." He looked up when Brigitte closed the locker door. "They said to go ahead to the classroom, because they're going to be late."

"Are they getting mobbed by fans?" Brigitte asked, catching his elbow to lead him while he continued to text.

"They're being asked to sign autographs and pose for selfies."

Brigitte burst out laughing. "Didn't see that coming. Aalia's probably managing okay, but I can't see Ruhul loving that attention."

"It's too bad, because he's kind of a natural at the modeling thing," Hēi Māo pointed out. He'd needed minimal coaching on the catwalk, and his photos from the shoot the next day were outstanding. "Pierre's probably going to try to recruit him."

"People don't mob **you** very often," she pointed out.

He rolled his eyes. "Not anymore, because they're terrified you'll eviscerate them if they touch your familiar." He grinned. Being out as a familiar had done some nice things to his modeling interactions. Though maybe it had more to do with who his witch was. "I used to have a bodyguard with me whenever I left the mansion, and he had to forcibly haul away squealing giggly girls who were trying to jump me on a pretty regular basis."

Brigitte's stared at him, her expression horrified shock. Suddenly her hand was on his arm and she was peering into his face in concern. "Did that bother you? Are you okay?"

"I'm fine, Gitte," he told her gently. He leaned on their classroom door to push it open. "I'm not an attention whore, like some models, but I didn't mind it so much. It was one of the few times anyone ever touched me, so..." He shrugged.

She scowled and stomped up the two stairs to her seat.

Oops. Reminding her that he spent most of his pre-familiar life touch-starved was one of those things he tried to avoid. "You okay, Gitte? I'm sorry if that upset you."

"I hate your father," she growled.

He reached over and patted her hand. "That's fair."

Aalia was laughing when she and Ruhul came in to the room a few minutes later. "Rhu has a fan club!"

Juniper chittered. "My boy is lovely. I'm pleased people finally noticed."

Hēi Māo smiled and patted his friend's shoulder. "Maybe we need to stick together to protect you, too. But Juniper's not wrong."

"Ugh," Ruhul groaned rubbing at his face. "My ma is all in a tizzy about how absolutely handsome I was, and my brother can't get past the idea that I've worn makeup several times now."

"I'm sorry, Rhu," Brigitte called. "I didn't really expect those consequences."

He turned to look up at her. "For you, Gitte, I am willing to suffer the indignities, but seriously. Cat-dude, how do you tolerate this on the regular?"

"I get paid a lot," Hēi Māo pointed out. "Kinda makes up for it."

"You two should all be getting your checks in the next few days," Brigitte said quickly. "Pierre wanted professional-grade models, which means he budgeted for that. You and Aalia did so well at the proposal show, he actually suggested keeping you for the real deal. He was pretty busy with his own business and I wanted to pick the models myself, anyway, and he was fine with that as long as Hēi Māo vetted their skills."

"Wait-wait-wait," Ruhul said, smashing the words together. "We're getting paid for working for you?" He suddenly looked a lot happier than he had earlier.

"You're getting paid well for your work," Brigitte corrected. "Not Hēi Māo's rate, but well above the usual beginner range."

"Does that make the fan-girls a bit more tolerable?" Aalia asked.

"Actually, it does." He shrugged. "I mean, I still would have done it for free, for you Gitte." He threw a finger-gun in her direction.

"You're an amazing friend," she said. "Thank you."

"Like I said, I'd do nearly anything for you." He dismissed her comment with a wave. "And I get to put the music stuff in my progressive and my portfolio, so you actually helped me out a lot too."

"Pierre really liked your style," Hēi Māo said. "You could probably get more modeling gigs if you wanted them." He covered his laugh as his friend's dark eyes went wide.

"Dude, I'm not sure I'm cut out for that." Ruhul's voice was a strangled whisper.

"Just let me know if you change your mind," Hēi Māo said. "It could be a good side job for lining the piggy bank, while you're getting your real career going."

Brigitte slouched at her desk beside Hēi Māo's cat tree, putting the final touches on her Mandarin homework. He'd finished his work, and lounged within arm's reach in his hammock. While he'd been very supportive of her insane work schedule, picking up her shifts in Nikli to allow her time to sew, there was a limit to what he'd been able to do over the last few weeks.

She was hoping to get to bed a little early tonight because she'd definitely been pushing herself a bit too hard. Her arms felt heavy, weighted down, and her eyes were so dry. The two months leading up to the show had been packed with late nights and more work than was humanly possible.

Fortunately she wasn't merely human, and she had an amazing familiar. But even magic-spiked energy drinks and fatigue banishing spells lost their effect after a while.

Hēi Māo was better caught up on everything than she was, with the exception of his progressive. She knew he was struggling to come up with a plan, but being a new student to L'Étoile du Nord while also being new to regular school, made it extra hard. And that didn't take into consideration the fact that he'd been so controlled by Pierre that he'd never even considered future plans. She kept insisting he'd gone through greater change than anyone else at school, and he didn't need to stress over the assignment. He didn't really agree.

Their phones buzzed, announcing an incoming text. She groaned and continued her work. She ignored the next two notifications, slowly pushing her braids back over her shoulder when they dropped onto her hanzi worksheet.

"Merp?" Hēi Māo chirped, leaning toward her from his sling.

"Hmm?" Resting her elbow on the desk, she turned and propped up her head as she looked at him. "What is it, Kitty?" She reached out and lightly touched the soft fur under his chin.

His eyes closed and he hummed. Then he pushed against her hand as he slithered out of his hammock onto the desk. Trotting over her homework, he went to the spot where his things were neatly stacked. He batted at his cell phone until it woke, then slid his paw over the screen, somehow managing his log-in pattern with his pink toe beans. He tilted his head as he read through the texts, just as another came in.

He let out a startled noise and dropped off the desk, shifting before he hit the ground. "You're gonna want to see this."

Brigitte stared at him for a moment. Even in his human form he was graceful, like a cat, and he wasn't given to abrupt or random transformations like that. She marveled over how cool it looked, once again impressed with his abilities. Then his words sank into her weary mind.

She straightened up sharply, knocking a book off the desk with a thump. "What is it? What's wrong?"

He had a curious smile on his face, like he wasn't quite certain how to feel. "Mayor Marchand called a special meeting of the Council of Paris." He glanced back at the phone in his hand. "He's... it looks like he's trying to help shape-shifters."

Mayor Marchand had never been one to rock the boat, so this came as a complete surprise. Brigitte pulled her laptop out of the pile of books and coursework, rushing to find a live cast of the news. Her exhaustion had been pushed back by adrenaline, which meant it would come back twice as hard.

"Who's texting? Is it Aalia?" She was naturally the most connected to current events.

"Ruhul." She saw Hēi Māo shake his head out of the corner of her eye, his messy blond hair flopping about. "He's with her at the press conference, and he's sending updates when she tells him to."

She wasn't quite revived enough to laugh, but she could see the humor in the scenario. Aalia barking orders at him as she took frantic notes, her hand up in the air to ask questions. She found the transcript in process, posted under a live video of the event.

The headline announced, "Mayor Marchand Declares War on Biased Statutes." That definitely could have been worse, but this station was known to be less inflammatory and divisive than others. She skimmed through the transcript, relieved that recent accessibility acts had resulted in live transcription at big events like this. Listening to their pompous mayor could be grating. It was easy to see where his daughter Celeste had picked up some of her behaviors. He took credit for everything, spent a great deal of time posturing, and in the end tended to avoid any words or actions that could provide ammunition to his detractors.

"He wants the council to review and remove old laws that do not serve a purpose in a modern and enlightened city..." she summarized what she was reading. "Oh." Many of the statutes on the list had been discussed by Aalia and Madame Chien in their recent *Miraculous Morph* article. In fact, every single statute under review involved the control or supervision of shape-shifters' actions and lives.

"So this... is good, right?" Hēi Māo asked, still looking uncertain. His understanding of ancient French and world governments was much more comprehensive than his grasp of modern politics.

Brigitte nodded. "It is. But I'm **really** not sure where it's coming from. Mayor Marchand's entire career has involved not upsetting anyone. Which, of course, is a very mediocre management plan." Maman and Papa had been very critical of his effectiveness in the past. "It avoids mass outrage, but often results in a low-level dissatisfaction from everyone. There's really no way to make everyone happy, and he's often more of an obstacle to change than anything else." She shook her head.

"Oh yeah," Hēi Māo agreed. "I hadn't really thought about that."

"It's like Marchand suddenly acquired a conscience or something. And if that were the case, I would have expected him to go after something else." Given his track record, he should have gone after an issue that would give him a lot of support from the more populated arrondissements. "The environment or possibly transportation in Paris would have made more sense because so many people want to see improvements there." Supporting shape-shifters was a pretty risky career move for him.

Another message announced its presence. "Ruhul says they're wrapping up, but one of the arrondissement mayors pulled Aalia aside to speak with her." He looked up from his phone again. "Why would she want to speak to Aalia?"

Brigitte rubbed at her face, trying to get her brain to cooperate, but she was just too tired to think this through. "Maybe they want to talk to her about *Miraculous Morph*. I mean, she just reported on several of these laws and how they impacted shape-shifters." She let out a huge yawn, feeling her jaw stretch uncomfortably.

"Why don't you take a nap," he suggested. "I'll keep an eye on the news, and anything Ruhul sends us."

"I still have homework." She gestured to the desk. "Just a little Mandarin. I should get it done."

Hēi Māo shook his head. "You'll do better with your homework if you rest now." He reached over and gently pushed the worksheet away. "If you don't catch up on your sleep, you're going to get sick. Worse, you won't be able to handle all the commissions you'll be getting as we go into the summer."

She snorted, but he had a point.

"Come on," he said, encouragingly. "You can finish up when we're at Master Fu's later for my lesson."

"Oh," she said, suddenly remembering. "He's starting you on chi patterns tonight, isn't he?" She liked to pay attention to his lessons, but finishing her homework there wouldn't take long.

"Yes." He rolled his eyes. "Now stop getting distracted. I'm your familiar. I know what you need right now. Let me do my job." He stood up and pulled back the covers on his bed, patting the mattress invitingly. "It's nap time."

"It's not a job," she insisted, but she'd already given up. His argument was too good, and she was just too tired to care. She stood and walked the short distance to his bed, relieved that she didn't have to climb the ladder to her own just now.

"True," he agreed. "It's more of a calling."
"You're ridiculous." She smiled and shook her head.
"I'm a cat. What do you expect?"

## *Chapter Sixteen*

Hēi Māo was putting his things in his backpack at the end of the day when Lucie approached his desk. "Did you need something?" he asked. Despite sharing most of their classes for nearly six months, he barely knew her. She'd been Celeste's only friend for several years, but she hadn't been there when Celeste attacked Brigitte mere days after he became her familiar. Lucie kept her distance, even after his witch made it clear that she didn't hold Lucie responsible for Celeste's cruelty. He wasn't sure if she was uncomfortable with him because he was a shape-shifter, or because her best friend had nearly killed him with magic before starting court ordered treatment.

"Oh, I... I have a letter for you and Brigitte." She held up a large yellow envelope, holding it close to her chest. "It's from Celeste."

He stared at the envelope, curious; he was a cat at heart, after all. They hadn't heard from his childhood friend since her apology back in November. *We have mail*, he told Brigitte. *Is it safe for me to touch?*

"You don't have to take it," Lucie said quickly, sounding flustered. "She didn't think you'd would want to hear from her, but she... wanted to try anyway."

"What's this?" Brigitte asked, having abandoned her own backpack to come down the steps.

"It's for you and Hēi Māo, from Celeste," Lucie explained. "She asked me to deliver it to you when I visited yesterday." She looked down at her fingers splayed over the yellow paper. "She'll understand if you want me to return it to her, unread."

He heard Brigitte's soft sigh. "May I check it, make sure it's safe?" she asked holding one hand as though ready to pluck the envelope from Lucie's fingers. "We have a history, after all."

Lucie held the envelope out, nodding eagerly. "Definitely. I'm sorry, I should've suggested that first."

He felt the barest stirrings of Brigitte's magic, and then it was gone, like a faint scent on a breeze.

"I'll take the letter," Brigitte said, slipping it out of the other girl's hand. "How are you holding up? It must be hard having your best friend so far away. Is she able to call or message you at all."

"Technology is restricted. They see it as a distraction to recovery." Lucie shook her head. "It **is** hard. And lonely." She shrugged. "But that second part is my own fault."

"Why is it your fault you're lonely?" Hēi Māo asked. There was so much he didn't understand about social rules and situations. His homeschool education had left him more than prepared for *lycée* academics. But being an isolated model, son of a fashion mogul, had only prepared him for business meetings and after-parties. He could network like a pro, but he still didn't get how the whole friend thing worked.

Lucie gave him a sad smile, and he had the vague feeling that she pitied him for not understanding. "I stood by Celeste while she was horrible to other people. I benefited from everything she got for herself as a result of bullying our classmates." She shrugged again. "She wasn't always a great friend, but I didn't think anyone else wanted me anyway."

"Do you want to join us for lunch tomorrow?" Brigitte asked.

Hēi Māo suspected his witch could not have surprised the other girl more if she'd tried.

"You'd let me have lunch with you?" she asked in a very small voice.

Brigitte nodded. "You've stayed friends with Celeste through some pretty tough stuff. You've proven you know how to be a good friend. It might be nice for you to be able to expand that beyond just one person."

Lucie smiled, looking more cheerful than Hēi Māo had ever seen her. "I'd love that." She looked at the envelope, nodding her head toward it. "I may not be as useful as Celeste, but what she says in that letter, it speaks for me, too."

They didn't get around to opening the envelope until they'd completed what little homework they had for the day. Their school work was lightening up as they moved toward revision and exams. This meant Brigitte had gotten caught up on sleep, and Hēi Māo was glad to see her looking more like her usual self; she'd even started a new design over lunch.

"Shall we see what Celeste has to say?" she asked, slipping the envelope out from between a couple of books.

"I'd like to know how she's doing," he said. He hoped she could find her peace, becoming closer to the girl he'd known. She'd never been as giving and kind as his witch, very few people were so genuinely good, but she hadn't been a self-obsessed brat, either.

"Would you rather open it yourself?" Brigitte asked, freezing with her fingers tucked under the flap. "Do you want to read it first?"

He shook his head. "No. You can do it." He thought for a moment. "It's probably safer if you open it, anyway." He'd started having difficulty containing his power of misfortune in the last week. He'd been doing all the exercises, practicing the way Master Fu suggested, without much success. It had even disrupted his tentative ability to see people's chi patterns. He wondered if it was because Brigitte had been too tired to fully function as his surge protector, but he wasn't one-hundred percent convinced that was the problem. Unfortunately, Master Fu was in Anyang, China for a conference this week. Hēi Māo hoped the tortoise shape-shifter would have some answers when they met up for his lesson over the weekend.

Brigitte ran her finger along the flap, breaking the seal. The envelope contained a folded yellow piece of paper, a perfect match for the envelope. A packet of white papers slid out onto the desk when she upended the envelope. She handed him the packet while she opened the letter.

He paged through them, not bothering to read the details just yet. He found a calendar, several pages of names and contact information, and a timeline on extra long paper that needed to be unfolded. He turned back a few pages to look more closely.

"Holy crap," Brigitte whispered.

He looked up from the contacts, all high profile people with at least part-time residence in Paris. He'd met many of them when representing Parenteau. "What is it?" he asked. Did he need to worry?

"Celeste is offering to help us in support of shape-shifters," she said, continuing to read.

"How much can she do while she's in treatment?" he asked.

"More than I would have ever guessed," Brigitte replied. "**She**'s the reason Mayor Marchand held that press conference, why he's trying to get the Paris Council to fix the laws."

He blinked a couple of times. "Wait. What?"

She waved the yellow letter at him. "She's trying to be a better person, and to make up for the wrongs she's done." She shook her head and let out a mirthless laugh. "She picked on me more than anyone else at school. Then she tried to use harmful magic against me and nearly killed you, her childhood friend in disguise. I guess she feels she has a lot to make up for." She handed him the letter.

He glanced at the flowing cursive, seeing the central paragraph where she explained that she and her papa had a lot of work to do to fix their relationship. She'd asked him to prove his sincerity by doing something truly good for a change.

"She won't be in treatment forever," Brigitte said. "She could get out as early as September."

"She's probably bored and lonely, too." He hadn't given her much thought in the past few months, and to be fair, he had his own things going on. "It's given her something to do that she can honestly feel good about."

Brigitte nodded. "I'm going to need to think about this."

"Because you don't trust her?" he asked. It was reasonable not to. They had a history that might just be too hard to get past. After all, he didn't trust his own… Pierre.

"Oddly, no." Brigitte looked surprised at her own reaction. "She has connections, and she knows how to present an image… honestly, if we could get Aalia to work with her, the two of them could be a devastating public relations team."

"Will Aalia be able to do that?" he asked. Her dynamic with the spoiled girl hadn't been much better than Brigitte's.

Brigitte sighed heavily. "We might need to build some bridges first." She picked up the stapled packet. "We should probably go visit her, start trying to see if we can work together without our past coming back to haunt us." Shaking her head, she put the packet down. "If I can work with her, Aalia will be willing to try."

"And don't forget Lucie," Hēi Māo said. "She must've been there when Celeste was writing this, or they talked about it. Remember what she said before she left?"

"She's on board…" Brigitte said softly, as if remembering. "You're right." She stood up and walked across the room, wandering aimlessly. He'd noticed that she often needed physical activity to get over a thinking block. Doodling could only help so much. He honestly felt the walk to her various favorite creativity haunts was more effective than the places themselves.

"What are you thinking, Gitte? How can I help?" he asked. At this stage in brainstorming, there were no obvious answers. Sometimes she needed a snack, or silence, or video games. Other times she needed to talk things through or spit out all her ideas to review afterward.

"I know how to work with the four of us." She gestured between them. "And a few random people here or there for a single event, like the fashion show, doesn't throw me off. But… for this to be successful, we're going to **need** to involve more people." She frowned. "Social change won't happen if it's just you, me, Ruhul and Aalia."

He nodded. "Probably not."

"I don't know how to manage all that." She looked vaguely panicked. "The show was actually about the limit of people-herding I can manage."

He grinned. "You did great, you know."

She stopped and stared at him. "Thank you."

"But I think you have more than enough on your docket without adding more," he said with gentle firmness. They were wrapping up the school year, but summer break wasn't long enough, and he expected her to be very busy with Butterfly. Next year was *terminale.* Studying for *le bac,* their university qualification exams, would need to take a much higher priority than homework did now. "I don't want you to take on more than you can handle, Gitte." Seeing her overworked for the fashion show's rushed but necessary deadline made him uncomfortable. Making that the norm was unacceptable.

The look she shot him was a mix of frustration and acceptance. "Yeah. I'm probably walking a tightrope there, aren't I?"

"Just a bit," he agreed. "And I'm glad you've realized it."

"I have," she admitted. "I'm just not sure how to... hmm."

"What?" He felt the tingle of her magic, warm and soft. Oh yeah. She'd just gotten an idea.

"I wonder if Celeste and Lucie might be able to help with the people side," she said. "Public relations and coordination." She chewed on her lower lip for a moment. "Want to go visit Celeste this weekend?"

He held out his fist with a thumb up. "Let's build us some bridges."

## *Chapter Seventeen*

Hēi Māo luxuriated in the feeling of all four legs pushed as straight as they could be while he arched his back. Morning stretch was one of the simple pleasures of life, right up there with sprawling in sunbeams, snuggles with his witch, and the light touch of her magic when she was inspired. He could feel the earliness of the hour in his bones as he rolled his shoulders, but he felt fresh and awake.

He leaned over Brigitte's pillow to peer into her face, careful not to brush against her with his whiskers lest that wake her. She had another interview yesterday that totally stressed her out. While she'd been doing better, she still needed to build her reserve back up before exams.

To avoid shaking her mattress, he stayed cat as he got up, using the stepped platforms she'd added to the wall for his dismounting convenience. They matched his cat tree and served as good perches as well as an easier route to the floor than the ladder when he had four shorter legs.

He shifted on his bed and opened his laptop to see if there

was anything he needed to be aware of. Aalia had helped him identify the best sources of reliable news, and she set up some filters to minimize the overload of information. If he was going to fulfill his role of managing the business side of Butterfly, he needed to be aware of anything in the news or on social media that mentioned Brigitte's company as well as big news in fashion. He also needed to know how Paris was responding to anything related to shape-shifters. It wouldn't be fair for his family and friends to work so hard for a cause that benefited him, if he wasn't engaged in it too. But he'd learned the hard way to approach that topic with caution. He also had to be careful not to let popular opinion weigh him down; it was so easy to feel like it was hopeless.

His email notification flashed at him in the upper left corner, demanding attention. He hit refresh on *Miraculous Morph*, and while it was loading he tapped to open his email.

His personal account had a message from the school's homework system with updates on his marks. Apparently several of his teachers had been up late last night catching up on grading. He opened the summary and sighed in relief. Mama and Papa had been wonderful, but he still got nervous about grades. Dr. Wheeler said it was anxiety. Pierre had not tolerated anything other than the very best. It helped that Brigitte was content with what she referred to as totally competent marks, and they weren't all at the top of the scale.

The Butterfly business account had several messages, something that still gave him a little thrill even though they didn't tend to require a lot of action on his part. Two were spam that hadn't been caught in the filter. One was a buyer who had missed the notice to contact Parenteau for the option to carry Shift. The last two each required an internet search to verify authenticity. He felt his excitement building as each check on his mental list was met in the affirmative. He grinned at the two requests for bespoke Shift commissions from well-known people. He knew this would happen, and his Brigitte was going to be so thrilled when she found out.

She deserved a celebratory breakfast.

*⁎<br>⁎⁎*

Brigitte wasn't surprised to wake up alone. Hēi Māo had been adamant about letting her sleep in whenever possible, and that wasn't a battle worth fighting. He could be surprisingly stubborn, but she had to admit he was also right in this particular instance. He was usually still in the room, at his desk or sitting on his bed when she got up, but he wasn't there.

Shivering as her body complained about the move out of her cozy bed, she snatched a sweatshirt from the hook on the corner loft support, and yanked it over her head. Her mind felt a little fuzzy and she had to think to figure out what day of the week it even was. She'd had a solo interview for a fashion magazine last night, and she couldn't even remember which one it had been. Clearly she'd been too busy and needed to take a little time for herself.

They'd tentatively discussed going to visit Celeste this weekend, but now she was thinking it would be better to take a break. She wasn't even sure when they'd last just taken time to relax and goof off. It felt like they'd been in a constant whirlwind of activity since winter break. Even game nights had turned into team meetings, addressing concerns and planning for the next week.

She was still considering what they might do with their day when she descended the stairs from her room. There was a flurry of activity off to her right, and she looked over to see Maman and Hēi Māo setting up the table. Flowers and a much more elaborate breakfast then they usually had, even on weekends, were laid out.

"What's going on?" she asked, searching her brain for some special event that she might've forgotten. It wasn't her anniversary of finding Hēi Māo, or them bonding. That wasn't until September and October. It wasn't her birthday. She was utterly stumped as she crossed the room.

Maman beamed at her. "My amazing daughter deserves a little spoiling now and then."

"Definitely," Hēi Māo agreed. He slid a plate of Nikli's finest breakfast pastries onto the table.

It was always trouble when the two of them conspired against her, though it was infinitely worse if her papa got involved. "Yes, and that's not at **all** suspicious."

Maman's laugh was a happy sound, relaxing Brigitte. "You know, Darling One, sometimes people who love you just want to take care of you. There's not always some ulterior motive."

"True." Brigitte nodded. Her family was very good at showing each other how much they cared, with both big and small actions. The same could be said for Aalia and Ruhul. But this just felt different. "You two have a guilty air about you," she said loftily, tilting up her nose. "I can tell when there's mischief afoot."

"I **am** mischief," Hēi Māo said. "Especially when I have four foots."

"Can't argue with facts," Brigitte said in agreement. "Though having you and Juniper together is just asking for trouble." She loved that while he shared her friendships, he had some of his own as well. Sure, she cared about Juniper, but they couldn't communicate and share the same way he could. Apparently, Hēi Māo and Juniper had had extensive philosophical conversations about the best way to support their witch-born. Juniper had been doing it long enough to have good advice and another perspective beyond Callie. But Hēi Māo had a better understanding of human nature and preferences, and their talks led to Juniper bringing Ruhul treats and morsels he could actually enjoy.

Hēi Māo patted the table, set for two. "Come eat. I'm sure you're hungry. It's nearly eleven."

"I'm just going downstairs to help Nik," Maman said. "Afternoon rush should be starting soon."

"Do you need either of us?" Brigitte asked. She didn't particularly want to work at Nikli today, nor did she want to give up time with her familiar, but the compulsion to show her parents how much she appreciated their support was strong.

Maman shook her head. "You two have the day off, remember? We planned it." Her smile was smug. "Besides I suspect you'll be far too busy. We'll be a bit late this evening, though. We have two new staff coming in for training."

"Oh. I didn't realize you'd actually decided to hire anyone." Brigitte felt a little guilty about that. Before she'd had a familiar she had helped her parents run the shop. Hēi Māo had started working shifts over the winter, and things ran very smoothly until she needed to start making multiple designs on a short timeline. Recently her parents had been talking about hiring someone to help with the counter.

"Our business is booming and your career is starting to take off," Maman said, a big smile on her face. "And we wouldn't have it any other way. Nik and I always knew this would happen eventually."

"Are you sure it's okay?" Brigitte asked. She couldn't help but feel like she had somehow betrayed her family.

Maman crossed the room and gave her a firm hug. "Of course it's okay." She stroked Brigitte's hair the way she always did when Brigitte was sad or nervous. "And the timing is really good. We've been able to find some excellent helpers who are really motivated."

"They're shape-shifters," Hēi Māo added with a grin. "I helped interview them."

Brigitte shook her head, confused. "When did this happen? **How** did I miss it?"

Maman laughed again. "You were deep in the throes of your

fashion show, Darling One." She patted Brigitte's shoulder. "No worries. I promise this is a good thing."

She watched her maman go out the apartment door, listening to her light steps on the stairs. It wasn't until Hēi Māo caught her hand that she remembered she was hungry.

"Come have breakfast. You'll feel much better," he promised.

She looked down at his large hand wrapped around hers, and realized she could feel excitement radiating off him. "I still think you're up to something."

"Of course I am," he agreed, gently tugging her to the table. "And once you've eaten something, I'll even share it with you."

Rolling her eyes, Brigitte took her usual chair and looked over the veritable feast on the table. "I hope you're going to help me with this. There's no way I can eat all of it." They were going to have leftovers, even if he helped, but those always made good quick snacks.

"I was waiting for you," he said. "I ate alone often enough to know that it's nicer to eat with someone."

"Are you sure I can't punch your father in the face?" she asked, taking a boiled egg from the bowl.

"I'm sure you could, but I'd rather you didn't."

Once her plate was loaded with everything she could possibly want, and more than she could probably fit into her stomach, she looked across the table at Hēi Māo. "Are you going to share yet?"

He shook his head. "You have to actually **eat** the food, not just look at it."

She swallowed her laughter and let out a completely fake indignant gasp. "I'm feeling so called out here. I just came to have breakfast."

"I've caught on to your wicked ways, Gitte," he said smoothly as he filled his plate as well.

It wasn't until she'd eaten the egg, some yogurt and half the

Danish, along with most of a cup of tea that he set his silverware down. He looked at her, and something about the way he waited felt significant.

"So have I earned my news?" she asked, arching her eyebrows.

He nodded. "Two very special commission requests came in to Butterfly just this morning," Hēi Māo said, looking smug. He'd been insisting for the last two weeks that she'd be making more clothes much sooner than she expected, and she'd disagreed.

"**Two** of them?" she said in surprise. She'd been gradually creating additional designs to add to the shift line, in case it was successful, but she hadn't sewn a single stitch since the show. It was a nice recovery period, and apparently it had come to an end. And the way he was drawing it out, these were clearly not the kind of commissions she usually got.

He nodded. "Are you familiar with the artist Zara?" he asked.

The name sounded familiar, but she couldn't quite pin it down. She'd probably heard about them in art class, but what was their medium? Paint didn't feel right. Neither did clay. She shook her head. "I know I've heard the name, but I can't place it."

Hēi Māo retrieved his laptop from the living room. He made space for it on the table, opened it, and clicked around with the touchpad. "You might recognize her work." He turned the screen toward her.

"Oh yeah! We learned about her in art class." Her sculptures were amazing and lifelike, beautiful bronze women who looked like they could simply walk out of the exhibit. Many of them appeared to be draped in fabric that was so realistic viewers were perpetually tempted to touch. She pointed to one. The woman stood on one leg, her opposite arm up in the air while a sheet of white rose up in a ruffled plume off her hip into the air. Her classmates thought it was a wave of water, but Brigitte was sure it was fabric from the way it flowed and draped. "That's my favorite. It's so dynamic."

"She's got a new exhibit opening at the Bozar Centre for Fine Arts in Belgium in two months, late July, and she'd very much like a unique piece consistent with the Shift line," Hēi Māo explained.

Brigitte couldn't hold back the happy squeal. "A world-famous artist wants **me** to make her something to wear for her next opening?" She stood up from her chair and danced around in a little circle. "Oh my gods! This is so amazing."

"This is why I couldn't tell you before you ate," Hēi Māo said, chuckling. "There's going to be no keeping you still long enough to eat now."

"But... why would she pick me?" Brigitte asked coming to a sudden stop. She loved her designs, but she hadn't really expected other people to feel very strongly about them. Sure, she'd hoped they would like them enough for stores to carry them, but she hadn't hung all her hopes on that. And famous people, who could basically pick their designer, choosing her was... well a fantasy, really. It was something she'd aspired to reach for eventually, not something she expected to happen while she was still in lycée.

"Two reasons," Hēi Māo said holding up two fingers. "You're awesome, obviously, and the only right choice for someone as artistic as her."

"Pffft! As if," Brigitte retorted with a laugh.

"The second reason is even better," he said, looking terribly pleased with himself. "Her email says that you inspired her; seeing your designs in action sparked an idea she can't let go of."

She'd inspired someone else?

"Zara sees beauty in everything; I can kind of see that in her art. And she's planning a new series of sculptures that she hopes will capture both sides of shape-shifters." He shrugged. "Not sure how, but that's her job."

Brigitte felt as though someone had yanked the rug right out from under her feet. She sat down heavily in her chair, staring at him in shock.

*Are you okay?* he asked, his voice gentle in her mind.

She nodded, not really capable of words.

*Are you really that surprised?* He got up and moved to sit beside her in his usual seat for family meals. *I told you you're amazing. You're so creative, and like Zara, you see beauty and magic everywhere. Of course she's going to feed off that creative energy.*

*I feel like I'm in a dream*, she whispered back to him.

*Is it a good dream?* he asked as his hand settled on her back between her shoulder blades.

*The best.* She felt choked up, and she wouldn't be at all surprised if her eyes started to leak. Getting a commission this big was a huge deal to her. It was a sign that she was being taken seriously as a designer and an artist. But actually inspiring another artist's work was more than she'd hoped for.

"Good. You deserve the best." He leaned in to rub his cheek against her shoulder. "Are you ready to hear about the other commission? Or do you need some more time to adjust?"

In the surprise, she completely forgotten that he'd mentioned that there were two. She took a deep breath, locked her fingers together, and nodded.

"Okay, the second commission is for Perci, the pop star from the Czech Republic. They've been getting huge in Europe and they have a tour coming up that'll take them to the US and Canada in the fall."

"Oh wow." She felt excitement building in her body again. She was familiar with Perci, having several of their songs in the peppy playlists she used for dancing, cleaning, and energizing herself. "What are they looking for?"

"They also want something consistent with the Shift collection, but with a little twist," he explained. "They want something that can convert from a masculine design to feminine design. And they'd like to debut it at the August music festival here in Paris. That's actually going to be the tour launch."

That **was** a twist, and she wasn't quite sure how to make it work yet, but she really wanted to try. Perci had come out as non-binary well before their music gained popularity, and they were known to drastically change looks between sets at concerts. Brigitte had seen video clips of them in sparkly dresses and sharp suits. They were able to pull off both looks incredibly well, and she wanted to find a way to truly showcase that ability.

"I should talk to each of them... find out what they're comfortable with... see if there's anything specific they're hoping for." Brigitte thought for a moment. "I probably need to come up with a list of standard questions to help get these kinds of things started."

"I can help with that," Hēi Māo offered. "I'm in touch with a few folks over at Parenteau who can give me some tips on what would make that easier for you. Checklists of fabrics, accents, that sort of thing. It wouldn't do to give someone sequins when they're looking for beads, or satin when they want silk."

She nodded. "That would definitely help." She took a deep breath. "We should set up a video meeting with each of them to discuss this a little further before we commit." She was glad she'd already had enough smaller scale clients, that she had an idea of how to proceed.

"I'll send emails after breakfast to get their availability," Hēi Māo said. "And I'll hit up my contacts."

Brigitte nodded. "Then I think we need to do some hard core relaxing this weekend. I know we talked about seeing Celeste, but..."

Hēi Māo shook his head. "I agree completely."

Brigitte smiled. "So we'll visit Master Fu this afternoon and see if he has suggestions to help you. Then… how about we go do something fun that you haven't ever gotten to do before, and we wrap up with movie night?"

"Should we invite Ruhul and Aalia?" he asked. "We had to cancel game night for your interview."

"Yeah," she agreed. "And tomorrow we'll have some witch and familiar bonding time."

He sighed, a contented smile on his face. "Purrrfect."

# Chapter Eighteen

Master Fu's smaller treatment room had soothing Chinese watercolor paintings and simple focus patterns on the walls. Hēi Māo sat on a cushion in front of his mentor while Brigitte waited on a little stool at the very edge of the room, near the wood and paper pocket door. He knew she liked being able to observe so she could understand his magic better, but she also didn't want to interfere unless she was needed. They worked on individual and joint magic together at home; this was his opportunity to learn from a master who understood his kind of power.

"Breathe in," Master Fu murmured. "Nice and slow."

The meditation exercises had helped him with a lot of things, including assignments from Dr. Wheeler and managing nightmares.

"Very good," Master Fu praised. "You have a much better grasp of your magic than you did when we started."

Hēi Māo smiled, feeling good about that. "But it's… it's been harder to control lately. I feel unbalanced."

"Brigitte mentioned that," Master Fu said. "She was wondering if she'd become less effective as your circuit breaker."

"Yeah. That's what we were thinking, because we first noticed it when she was so exhausted." He didn't like the other ideas that crept into his head at night. The ones that suggested he wasn't suitable as her familiar and that he was going to harm her somehow.

"That's possible, but I don't think that's all there is to it." The old Chinese man rubbed at his beard, twirling his fingers in the wiry hairs. "Has it improved now that she's not run down?"

Hēi Māo wobbled his hand to suggest it hadn't changed much. He didn't like admitting it because it seemed to support his more awful theories.

"I think there are several factors at play here, young Tom. The first is that you became a familiar which has amplified your magic as much as it has Brigitte's."

Hēi Māo nodded. They knew that much. But things hadn't gotten out of control after they bonded. He hadn't really noticed any change in his power until January or February, and then it had been fine until April.

"But you didn't know how to properly access it until more recently," Master Fu continued. "Over the winter, you and Brigitte started training you to find and use it. I suspect that unlocked something, or rather it's more like it took the stopper out of the bottle containing your power, and you can't put it back in."

"That's **exactly** what it feels like," Hēi Māo said in agreement. "How do we put the stopper back in?"

Master Fu shook his head, a grim smile on his face. "We can't. You do not wake magic and then expect it to go dormant again simply because it's inconvenient. Many times, it just requires a bit of patience until you grow accustomed to the changes." He crossed his arms, his expression going contemplative. "I'm going to see if I can find any members of your family, the shape-shifting side. My power is protection, not misfortune. Relations and matched magics generally have the best success helping our kind find our way around our abilities. We will be able to get a handle on this, Tom. It may take a little longer than you'd prefer, but we'll get there."

"I don't like how it feels," Hēi Māo grumbled. "I'm afraid I'm going to lose control of it."

Master Fu gently patted his hand. "It may be uncomfortable for both of you, but I promise, Brigitte's magic won't let it get fully loose, and it won't hurt her. Your bond won't let it."

Brigitte didn't think anything of it when Hēi Māo slipped off the couch to the floor during the movie. He did it often enough, finding it comfortable to sit almost anywhere, regardless of his form. She dug her hand in the big popcorn bowl situated between herself and Aalia, without looking away from the television. They'd chosen The Tale of Princess Kaguya, an animated film from Japan. Hēi Māo was the only one who'd seen it, back when he'd been Jacque.

Hēi Māo's head settled on her knee, and she knew without looking that he was gazing up at her with a soft fondness in his green eyes. It was a look she'd been seeing a lot more often these days, and it made her feel all happy and warm. She felt him tilt his head back, and she glanced down to see his mouth open, wordlessly begging for popcorn. This had also become routine in both his human and cat shape, so she dropped two pieces of popcorn onto his tongue without thinking about it and turned back to the film.

Poor Little Bamboo, being forced to act as a lady and princess to please her father, when all she wanted was to run and sing. Though the bamboo cutter clearly loved his daughter and was doing these things because he wanted to give her the best life he could, it reminded her enough of Hēi Māo's situation before he ran away from home. Was it possible that Pierre had been doing the same?

Had he abused his son in a misguided and biased attempt to make his life better or safer?

Gnawing on her lip to distract herself from the painful path those thoughts could lead, she slipped her hand into Hēi Māo's soft blond hair, her fingers absently caressing his scalp in all his favorite places. She relaxed as the low rumble of his purr started up, instantly calming her.

"Hey Gitte?" Ruhul asked from Aalia's other side. "Can you turn up the volume a little?"

She leaned over to snatch the remote from the table where Hēi Māo's untouched orange juice sat. She tapped the button a few times, then offered the remote to her long-time friend from behind Aalia's head. "Here. In case you need more."

Ruhul took the remote and chuckled. "I can't quite hear over Cat-dude's happy sounds."

Brigitte smiled and looked back down at Hēi Māo, his eyes closed as he rubbed his face against her leg, his hands kneading and clinging to her calf. He wasn't watching the movie at all. When he got this far into pettings, as cat or boy, he usually lost all awareness of what was happening around him. Seeing him so relaxed and content melted away the last of her stress.

## *Chapter Nineteen*

Hēi Māo navigated quickly to the checklist he'd been working on for the last couple days. He and Brigitte would meet with Zara by video conference after school tomorrow, and they had Perci's consultation scheduled for late Friday night.

"Ric gave me a lot of really helpful advice," Hēi Māo explained as his witch moved her chair closer. "He's the designer I told you about. The one who handles all of Parenteau's initial requests for custom designs." Most of the questions had been relatively easy to convert into a checklist, a format that worked better than short answers for Brigitte's early stages of development. While he'd been waiting for Ric's information, he'd asked Brigitte what **she** thought would be most helpful. He'd been able to combine both concepts into a form that led with check boxes and finished with open-ended questions.

"Thanks so much for doing this," she said, brushing the back of his neck lightly.

He closed his eyes for a moment and let out a little hum. Even when she'd thought he was just a cat, all her gentle little touches made him feel important and loved. He hadn't wanted to give those up in either form, which resulted in an awkward conversation during one of their first joint sessions with Dr. Wheeler. They'd had to compromise to give him what he needed while still being appropriate. He'd gone from being almost never touched by anyone, aside from tailors, stylists, and the occasional grabby fan, to cuddles and pets as a cat. During one of their lunches with Madame Desmarais, he'd found out that shape-shifters had different touch needs than humans, depending on their animal form. He would have learned how to meet those while following regular social rules if he'd grown up with other shape-shifters. The woman been more than a little horrified the first time she'd seen him rub cheeks with Brigitte, his cat-influenced version of *la bise*.

"I like helping you," he reminded her. Just a few days ago, he'd worked with her on preparations for the coming Summer Solstice. As a witch-born high holiday, it was an important celebration. And like all other special occasions, it hadn't been observed in the Parenteau household once his mother went missing. The Defresne-Li family celebrated a variety of French, Chinese, and witch-born holidays. He'd loved their Winter Solstice, Lunar New Year, Spring Equinox, and May Day traditions, and was, perhaps, unreasonably excited for another holiday.

"I like it when we're able to work together on things outside of magic," Brigitte said. "I mean, I love working with you on magic, too, but it's nice that there's more to us than that."

"Yeah." He nudged his laptop to sit a little more directly in front of her. "Let me know if there's anything else you want me to add or change. I'll copy the final form over into those shared folders." He and Ruhul had set up a small network to serve as a backup and easy sharing space for all of Butterfly's work. It felt more secure than cloud storage, which made Brigitte more comfortable about having her designs and business contacts digital.

"I started files on both Zara and Perci. There's a presentation for each, assessing their outfits from the last eighteen months to give you an idea of their current styles and preferences." It had been another of Ric's recommendations to have examples of the client's past wardrobe for similar events. While Brigitte was preparing documentation for her progressive, he'd scoured the internet for photos and information about who Zara and Perci had worn and what criticism came from those appearances.

"Hēi Māo, Brigitte," Papa's voice carried up the stairs. "You have company."

"Were you expecting anyone?" Hēi Māo asked.

Brigitte looked surprised. "No. And I can't imagine who it would be." She fidgeted a moment. She'd been more nervous about surprises ever since Nikli was vandalized. "We'll be right down," she called back.

There were other voices, and he recognized one as Master Fu. "I don't think it's anything to worry about if Master Fu brought them."

She frowned, contemplative. "Well **that** just makes me curious."

"Yes!" He raised his fist in the air. "I'm finally rubbing off on you."

He was delighted when his words startled a laugh out of her. "Silly Kitty." She nodded to the computer where his introductory consult form was displayed. "I can't think of anything I'd change at this point. You were probably more thorough than I would have thought to be. Let's just start with these, and if we realize there are things that could make them better, we can change them in the future."

"Great." He pulled the keyboard closer and copied the form into Zara's and Perci's files. "We can get back to this later." He stood up. "Let's go see what Master Fu wants."

135

It was nearly evening, and the late spring sun touched everything in the living room with golden light. Papa was speaking with Master Fu and a couple. The woman was tall and willowy, with bobbed blond hair. The man was a little shorter, with a stockier build, and shaggy brown hair. A *collège*-aged girl, probably eleven or twelve years old, stood slightly behind them. She could easily be their daughter, and her pale green eyes idly wandered around the room, suggesting bored. Her honey-blond hair was up in two space buns.

"Good afternoon, Tom and Brigitte," Master Fu said, bowing slightly. "I hope I didn't interrupt anything too pressing."

Hēi Māo bowed in greeting, pressing his palms together. "Not at all, Master. We were just preparing for some meetings later this week."

"Meetings?" the woman asked, her interest clearly piqued. Her voice tickled a memory that he couldn't quite access.

Brigitte smiled her polite and cautious smile. "Hēi Māo and I run the Butterfly fashion house," she explained. "We had our first solo launch in April."

"Oh yes," the woman said, nodding eagerly. "We've been keeping up on all your public activities, and they've been **so** impressive."

Hēi Māo realized her eyes were the same color as his own.

"With just the two of you running it, how is your fashion house structured?" the man asked, sounding genuinely curious.

"Brigitte's the design genius, and I handle the business side," Hēi Māo said. If they were fans of Butterfly and didn't know that, he probably needed to look at their website's introduction and about pages to make it clearer. "I've still got a lot to learn, but Papa and Mama have been great mentors. And I'm signed up for a summer class to get a better understanding of some of the fashion-specific business elements."

There was a moment of silence, eventually broken by the girl. "Are you really my cousin?" she asked, tilting her head. "I mean, I've heard about you, but you don't really look like the pictures."

"I look different for pictures because my stylist – wait." He'd started explaining before his brain caught the meaning of all her words. "Cousin?"

Brigitte's hand slid into his, soothing him before he even realized he was having a melt down. "I'm sorry. Could we have introductions?"

Master Fu stepped forward. "My apologies for the surprise," he said gently. "I'd hoped it would be a pleasant one." He shot the girl an exasperated look. "With proper introductions of course."

The girl offered a sheepish smile, and Hēi Māo nodded numbly.

"This is Adalene Barbeau, Ysabeau's sister," Master Fu went on, gesturing grandly to the woman, his aunt.

No wonder her voice felt like a memory. While he'd never met any of Pierre's family, his maman had brought him around to see her relatives regularly. He'd met Aunt Adalene before, though it had easily been ten years since the last time, and his memory was a bit foggy on the specifics. He bowed to her.

"This is your uncle, Marcel Barbeau, and your cousin Iva," Master Fu continued. "Like you and your mother, they are cat shape-shifters."

"I understand you've started having trouble keeping your magic under control," Adalene said. "And shape-shifter magic training almost always comes easier with family."

Hēi Māo nodded, unsure how to respond, or if he even could.

*Do you need help?* Brigitte asked. *I don't want to speak for you, if you'd rather do it yourself.*

*I can't,* he managed to reply. *Please help.*

She squeezed his hand. "I'm sorry, this is a bit of a surprise for us, and while I promise, he's happy, he needs a moment to get comfortable with this."

He nodded his agreement.

"Hēi Māo didn't know he even had magic until he ran away from home last June," she explained.

He suddenly realized he was coming up on his one year anniversary of the photo shoot that changed his life. They'd been so busy it hadn't even occurred to him.

"He didn't know?" Adalene demanded, clearly appalled.

"Ysabeau disappeared when he was very young," Brigitte reminded her. "I'm not sure how it is for shape-shifters, but it was before the age most witch-born start formal training." She gave his hand another squeeze. "We don't know if his father even knew he had magic outside of his ability to shift. But it's possible that he deliberately mislead Hēi Māo to think he didn't have any." She shrugged. "Either way, he only started using it shortly before we bonded."

"I'm so sorry." Adalene closed her eyes and let out a heavy breath. This is so much worse than I could have imagined."

*Let's not tell her about any of the other things Pierre did to me,* Hēi Māo suggested. He wondered if she was as upset with him, as she was the situation. She may be family, but he didn't know her at all, and he'd learned the hard way that family could sometimes be the worst.

*Agreed.* "We started working with his magic, basic training exercises and such, over the winter."

Adalene nodded. "Why did you wait so long? He became your familiar in October or November, didn't he?" She shot Master Fu a look that could best be described as a glower. "Magic users without training are a danger to those around them."

"We couldn't start without a mentor," Brigitte explained, bowing to Master Fu. "That would have been foolish. And we waited until he was ready. He'd had some unpleasant experiences with magic in the past, and I didn't want to rush him."

"Those are both good reasons," Marcel said, gently laying a hand on his wife's arm. "We're so accustomed to young people who are rash with their magic. It's nice to see someone who thinks through consequences and plans to be safe."

Adalene's shoulders slumped and she nodded.

Iva let out a groan. "It was **one** time, Papa."

Brigitte giggled. "I made some rash decisions when I was younger, too," she admitted, smiling at his cousin. "But I learned from them."

"I have to get downstairs to help Ling close up Nikli," Papa said. "But we'd love to have you all stay for dinner."

"I'm afraid I must decline, as I must also return to my own shop for a late client," Master Fu said regretfully. "But I would love to enjoy your hospitality another time."

"We'd be delighted to have the opportunity to get to know you and your family, Nik," Marcel said. "Thank you so much."

Papa headed out with Master Fu.

"Won't you please have a seat?" Hēi Māo asked, relieved to finally have control over his voice again.

They sat, and the silence was awkward for a moment.

"We are so happy to be able to see you again," his aunt said, leaning forward in her earnestness.

"Did you tried to see me before?" Hēi Māo asked. It hadn't even occurred to him that his maman's family might have made an effort to see him after she was gone.

"Your father was quite firm about preventing that," Adalene replied. "He appeared to be under the impression that we would spirit you away to wherever we were hiding her." She shook her head sadly. "But he couldn't have been further from the truth."

He thought for a moment. "It doesn't surprise me he did that."

Pierre didn't trust anyone.

"From what Wang has told us, it sounds like you have Ysabeau's power," Adalene said, settling back on the couch, her hands folded in her lap.

"I think so." Hēi Māo nodded. "Misfortune."

She looked puzzled. "Are you quite certain it's misfortune?" she asked, tilting her head.

He was about to respond that he was, but then he realized he'd always been the one to call it that. He hadn't really known what he was doing when he discovered it. "Is there a test to confirm what it is?" he asked. "I always just thought of it that way, but... now I'm not so sure." He didn't like sounding so hesitant around someone he didn't yet know if he could trust. Brigitte's hand in the middle of his back instantly eased his worries.

"Ysabeau carried the power of destruction," Adalene explained, looking thoughtful. "But I think it would be pretty easy to mistake the two, depending on how you use it."

"Is that your magic, too?" he asked, hopeful.

Adalene shook her head. "My skill is illusion. However, your mother and I trained together. I learned a lot about her power as well as my own, and I'm sure I have some ideas to help you." She nodded happily. "Destruction magic is rare, and I'm not sure you'd find a more qualified teacher in all of Paris. Our old teacher no longer even lives in France, and there's no one as experienced with this power than I." Although her words could have come off as bragging, her tone suggested she spoke fact.

Hēi Māo glanced at Brigitte. *How common is creation as a magic talent?*

*Rare,* she replied. *Incredibly rare. I've never met another witch with creation magic.*

It was jarring to suddenly find that his magic may not be at all what he thought it was. Though it might explain why it was suddenly

140

so hard to manage. He wondered if having Brigitte's opposite was part of what made him such a good fit as a familiar for her.

"Why would destruction and misfortune be similar?" Iva asked, looking skeptical. "That seems… fake."

"Destruction can touch physical things as well as metaphorical or magical things," Adalene explained, freeing her hands to gesture gracefully as she spoke. "If he thought he carried misfortune, and therefore focused his magic on a person or object's fortune, he could destroy their good luck."

"So the end result would be the same because he was putting his destruction into their good luck?" Brigitte asked. The look she shot him was full of pride. *Clever Kitty!*

"Do we need to do anything to make sure my power is truly destruction?" he asked.

"Oh yes." Adalene nodded. "I'll be able to tell, if you're willing to work with me." She paused.

He wanted to try. He probably needed to know exactly what his magic was, but he wasn't sure he was ready to work with his aunt. It had taken weeks before he'd been comfortable working with Master Fu.

Brigitte's hand ran from his shoulder to his elbow a couple of times, soothing him. "Let's get to know each other just a little more, first," she suggested. "He hasn't worked with many magic users because some magic hurts him."

"That happens to me, too," Iva said quickly, as though she was pleased to have something in common with him. "Some witch-born magic is nice, but some is… it burns."

Hēi Māo nodded eagerly in return. "That's it exactly." It was nice to have someone who had felt the same thing. He knew Brigitte, Mama, and Papa believed him, but sometimes he felt like it was all in his head. "Brigitte's magic feels delightful. It's like lying in the perfect sunbeam on the softest carpet."

"Oh," Iva sighed. "That's so nice."

"Mama's and Papa's magic… uh that's Ling and Nik," he added when he realized they might not know who he was talking about. "Their magic is soft and gentle. But there are some people I can't even stand to touch because I can feel it in their skin and it…" He made a face. "It's really unpleasant." In the hallways at school, he'd discovered that it wasn't just Pierre's magic that hurt.

"See?" Iva said, looking at her mother expectantly. "It's not just me. I'm not just being hypersensitive."

"I never said you were, sweetheart," Adalene insisted. "But there's not much we can do about it."

"You should never just have to get used to being harmed by others' magic," Brigitte corrected firmly. "That's not acceptable."

Adalene sighed and looked skyward. "We live in Paris and she attends a large *collège.* Some touch simply can't be avoided."

"Oh, I agree there," Brigitte said. "But we should be able to mitigate her contact with ambient magic."

Hēi Māo grinned. "You're making a spell, aren't you?" It really wasn't a question. He'd felt the spark of inspiration.

Brigitte's focus turned inward, as she mumbled to herself. "We could put it on a shirt… but that's limiting. Maybe a ward?" She shook her head. "Too bulky. And we'd need someone with compatible magic to do the casting…"

Hēi Māo got up and found a partially used notebook in the cabinet under the television. "Here, Gitte." He opened it on the coffee table in front of her, slipping a pen into her hand. "She's going to need a moment. Does anyone want tea or something else to drink?"

\*\*\*

Hēi Māo sat down in the living room to work with his aunt Adalene. He'd agreed to try just enough to see what his power truly

142

was, as a test for if he could work with her in the future. His uncle Marcel readily went to the kitchen to help her parents with dinner preparations, and Brigitte brought Iva upstairs. It would give everyone the space they needed, and she could get to know Hēi Māo's cousin a bit. She was glad the chaos of the fashion show was well behind them, but she wished she'd done a little more tidying at her desk. She cared about what his family thought of her.

"You have the coolest room," Iva said, gazing around with wonder. She paused, looking critically at the twin and lofted bed. "You two share it?"

Brigitte nodded. "He **is** my familiar, and witches and familiars generally prefer to stay together. If he wanted his own room, we'd give him the guest room, but he wants to stay here with me." She had offered him his choice of accommodations, but after years isolated in an enormous bedroom, he'd been adamant about sharing. "When I found out he wasn't **just** a cat, we had a long conversation about how we wanted to move forward. He helped design our new shared space so it would be as much his as it is mine." She unhooked the privacy curtains around his bed, enclosing it. "It was really important to me that he feel comfortable and loved."

"How did you catch him?" Iva asked, settling stiffly on the chaise.

"I didn't." Brigitte was a little irritated to have to keep answering that question. She would have expected his family to do their research or, at the very least, watch the interviews online. "I was looking for a cat. My magic wanted a stray, but I would never force a cat to come to me or stay with me."

Iva looked puzzled. "He **came** to you, knowing you were a witch looking for a cat?"

Brigitte nodded. "He made it clear that he wanted to come home with me, so I brought him here. And we got to know each other for a while before he became my familiar."

Iva's green eyes, a shade lighter than Hēi Māo's, closed slightly, calculating. "Don't most witches bond immediately?"

Brigitte shrugged. "A lot of us do. But I wanted to be sure he knew what he was getting into, and that he really wanted it." She chuckled. "He got very impatient with me, and even started the bonding before the ritual."

"Oh." With that, Iva suddenly seemed to relax. "So he decided first."

Brigitte nodded, realizing the girl might just be watching out for her cousin. She could live with him having a few more people making sure he was safe and happy.

"Is it weird, sharing a room with a boy?" Iva asked, suddenly at ease.

"It was a little strange at first, I'm not gonna lie," Brigitte said, smiling. "He's a cat and a model. Absolutely no modesty or body shyness." She rolled her eyes and the younger girl laughed. They'd both had to make some adjustments. The changing screen was put in the corner, not that he needed it. "And I know it sounds really odd to a lot of people. But we'd already been sharing a room for over a month before I discovered I was living with a teenage boy." She snorted. "Not something I'd recommend doing with just **any** boy."

Iva cackled with glee. "My *mère* would completely freak out, and there's no way I'd be allowed to share a room with a boy. Ever. Maybe don't tell her about this just yet."

Brigitte nodded. She'd suspected that, and it wasn't something she advertised beyond their friends. Very few knew that Hēi Māo slept on her bed most of the time. If Adalene never came upstairs, she might assume there were two separate bedrooms up here, and there was no need to disabuse her of that notion.

"How much of your family's visit today was motivated by checking on Hēi Māo, and making sure he's being taken care of properly?" she asked. She would have laid odds on it being a significant factor.

Iva shrugged. "I know it's part of the reason we **all** came. I'm supposed to be finding out what kind of person you are," she confided. "Not that we could do anything about it anyway. He's your familiar, and even I know that means we couldn't take him away."

"Yeah," Brigitte said. "His father tried that and failed."

Iva grinned, showing off a small gap where she was still missing a tooth on the bottom left. "But we really wanted to get back in touch with him. We've been trying to keep up with everything he's been doing, and... *Mère* says he seems more content than he used to. She wanted to make sure we weren't wrong about that."

"That's fair, I guess," Brigitte agreed. "And if your mother can help him with his magic, it's a nice bonus."

"Well I can already tell I like you," Iva insisted. "You don't feel super fake like his *père*. Tom or Hēi Māo... what should I call him? Anyway, my cousin seems really happy."

"His new legal name is Tom, so that's a safe bet," Brigitte explained. "But people who are close to him can call him Hēi Māo, that's the name I gave him when I found him. Just don't ever call him Jacque." She thought for a moment. She was glad Iva liked her, but she felt like she owed the girl a little more reassurance. "Even when he was just a cat, it was really important to me that he was happy. I could tell he'd run away from his old home, and I suspected he'd been mistreated. I promise I want him to be as free and happy as he can be."

"My *mère* says his *père* is an asshole," Iva said, her voice quiet, like she was trying to avoid being heard from downstairs.

"She's not wrong," Brigitte said with a snort. She had several other unsavory words she used for Pierre on a regular basis. "Is there anything specific you want to see or do up here?"

Iva leaned back and looked at the crates full of fabric. "You weren't kidding about running a fashion company, were you?"

Brigitte smiled and crossed the room to pick up her current sketchbook. It had all the designs from the Shift collection, including several that hadn't made the cut for the show, and others that she had created since. "This is our current project." She held out the book. "I wanted to do something that promoted shape-shifters, that helped normalize the idea of people changing the way they look. We do it all the time with our clothes, or hair, or makeup. And if it's okay for witch-born and humans, it shouldn't be wrong for shape-shifters."

Iva's eyes went wide, and she reverently opened the sketchbook. "I heard about this, you know. We watched the show, and we **never** watch fashion stuff unless Tom's doing the runway." She paged through, eventually landing on the first design in the book that was used in the show, Brigitte's own convertible bubble dress. "Oh wow. I **love** this." She turned the sketch toward Brigitte. "**You're** the one who made this?" She looked more closely at Brigitte. "You wore it in your own show!"

It was nice to see how excited she was. "I did."

"This was huge, everyone was talking about it! Not just shape-shifters," Iva said, continuing through the designs. "I didn't realize it was made by a teenager, though, so it didn't really connect that Butterfly was **this**."

"Do you want to see pictures? I have those, too," Brigitte offered.

"Can I see some of Tom?" Iva asked. "I **know** he's a model, and I've been seeing him all over Paris on billboards since I was little." She wasn't quite dismissive. "And *Mère's* always told me he's my cousin that we could never meet because his *père* was such a complete piece of garbage. But... it's hard to see that guy I just met with the super fluffy hair, in those pictures."

"He **does** look different without all the makeup and hair gel," Brigitte cautioned. She went to a bin next to her fabric crates and pulled out a final copy of the lookbook from Shift's release. Pierre sent a carton of them to Brigitte when Parenteau shipped them to distributors and boutiques after the show.

She opened the front cover, displaying pictures from the photo shoot the day after the show. "Let's see," she said flipped through the pages. "Here he is." She handed Iva the lookbook, taking back the sketchbook.

Iva slowly looked through all the pictures, frequently returning to the ones that included Hēi Māo. "Wow. I can see him, the guy downstairs who's a little goofy? I see him in these now."

"These look more like his real face because I like my models to smile and look happy," she pointed out. "He really doesn't look the same when photographers require him to use a serious or brooding expression."

"Yeah, what's with that?" Iva demanded. "Why would I buy clothes from models who look bored or constipated?"

Brigitte laughed. "Tradition, I guess. But I've always wondered the same thing." She took the lookbook back and set it aside wondering if it was too soon to make a proposal. "So, I have an idea to help you with your magic sensitivity. The not-so-subtle irony is that it requires some magic. Is that something you'd be interested in trying? I mean, if other people's magic bothers you a lot, you shouldn't have to put up with it. There should be a way to fix it."

The younger girl chewed on her lip uncertainly. "It is really annoying. *Mère* doesn't realize how distracting it is, and there are a lot of witch-born in my class." She shook her head, and Brigitte could see it was something that had really bothered her. "But I think I'd have to have permission to do anything with magic."

"That's fair," Brigitte agreed. "But if your parents were okay with it, would you want to try? I mean, I'm already going to make something for Hēi Māo because he has the same problem, and it wouldn't be any trouble to make some for you, too. If my magic doesn't bother you, that is." Her earlier idea of making a barrier or ward to block unwanted magic had combined with her idea from a few months ago about the protection spray for clothing.

"Can you tell me a little more about it?" Iva asked.

"I'm thinking of a spray potion, something you can spritz over your skin, that would keep other magic from touching you," Brigitte said. "You'd probably have to apply it once a week... we'd have to test it a bit to see how long it really holds up. I haven't made it before, so I'm actually not sure how long it will last." She shrugged. "There will be some trial and error."

Iva's eyes were wide. "I had no idea potions like that existed."

"Well there's a lot of potions out there and a lot of different ways to deliver ambient spells." She'd grown up surrounded by them, after all. "But this potion is new. I've just invented it."

Iva stared at her, blinking a bit. "You **just** invented it?"

Brigitte nodded. "I got the idea when we were downstairs and you mentioned that a lot of magic was uncomfortable for you. Hēi Māo's that way, too. We're just really careful about crowds. At school, everyone knows he's a familiar, so no one touches him there."

"Is it normal to just make up potions and spells?" Iva asked. "I mean, none of my witch-born friends do that."

Brigitte felt her face go hot. "Well, no. It's not... it's not abnormal, though, either." She stopped a moment to gather her thoughts. She didn't like to advertise her talent, especially with people she didn't know well. "My parents always taught me to try new things and make new things. While they use a lot of the same enchantments and potions most of the time, they sometimes need to make new ones."

Iva nodded, clearly not satisfied.

"And my brain is just good at making things." She shrugged. "Umm, did you hear about Mademoiselle Butterfly?" She didn't like mentioning the event because it felt like bragging, and at the same time, it was horrible to remember.

"Pfft, I think all of Paris heard about... oh my gods." She started bouncing and waving her hands like she was a fledgling attempting her first flight. "That was you! You're Mademoiselle Butterfly, and your fashion company is Butterfly, and Tom rescued you when you almost drowned after you banished that nasty demon!"

Brigitte nodded, hoping she could redirect the girl before this got out of control. "Yeah. Well the spell I used to banish it, I made it up on the spot. I'd learned the basics to such things, but I had no interest in dealing with demons. I'm not going into magical law enforcement. So I didn't learn any actual spells for that kind of thing. Demons aren't a... common problem in modern Paris."

"Thank goodness," Iva said, giggling. "Can you imagine having to call in late to school because there's a demon hanging out on your street?"

"I do not want to live in that world," Brigitte replied instantly, shuddering for effect. "Anyway, I had to create something based on the magical concepts I knew," she explained. "I did the same thing when I created a potion for our clothes that counters harm. It works for small things, like someone intentionally dumping juice on you at school, or big ones, like an attack."

"You're really cool. You know that, right?" Iva asked. "You see a need and just, boom! You magic up a solution."

Brigitte smiled. "I like helping people, and I feel like it's my responsibility to use my magic to help."

"Am I going to be allowed to come just to see you?" Iva asked, her forehead furrowed and her head tilted to the side just a little.

Brigitte nodded. "I'd love that. Most of my cousins are in China, and I don't get to see them very often." She thought her kitty would like seeing some of the family he'd been deprived of.

"Hey," Brigitte said softly, spinning her chair to face him. "Are you okay?"

Hēi Māo shrugged. They sat together at their desk, and he struggled to pick up where they'd left off before his relatives showed up. The unexpected lesson in destruction magic had been overwhelming, and he wasn't sure what to think. "Is it bad?"

"Is what bad?" she asked, clearly confused.

"My magic?" Misfortune hadn't bothered him. It seemed to explain some of the crappier elements in his life, and it wasn't too dangerous. At least not until he started having trouble controlling it. Destruction was another thing all together.

"Why would it be bad?" she asked, her hands reaching to cup his face.

"It's not safe," he pointed out. His aunt had been adamant that he needed to be cautious about using his power, something Master Fu had never been concerned over. "I'm not safe. I could hurt you." He really hated that his fear had been valid all along.

"Creation can be just as dangerous," she insisted. "Unchecked creation is how we get cancer." She slid one hand into his hair, soothing him despite himself. "And just like how my magic can't accidentally harm you, yours can't harm me."

"I don't want to hurt **anyone**." He hated the whine in his voice and the insecure weak way he felt.

"And you won't," she promised. "I'm still your shut-off valve, okay?" She hugged him, pulling his head down to her shoulder. "If anyone had to have the power to destroy, I'm glad it's you. You're compassionate and won't just throw it around. You'll be responsible with it. I can trust you."

He closed his eyes and relaxed against her. If she trusted him, he'd be okay.

## Chapter Twenty

The Jeanne d'Arc Youth Arcane Abuse Rehabilitation Center was not at all what Hēi Māo expected. It felt, and smelled, nothing like a hospital, and it bore no similarity to the detention centers he'd seen on television. Residents had private bedrooms, but shared space for dining and socializing. It had more of a communal apartment or dormitory vibe than a state-run institution. When he thought about it, it probably made sense. Emotionally healthy people didn't generally use magic to harm others. Most of the kids and teens sentenced to stay here were recovering from some form of abuse or neglect. They needed comfort and healing, something he understood much better than he used to.

"I must say," said the woman who led them through a series of locked doors. "It's nice to see someone else taking an interest in Celeste's well-being."

Hēi Māo shot Brigitte a surprised look. "I know Lucie comes every Thursday," he said.

"Yes. And the mayor stops in every other Monday," the woman continued. "But she's had no one else at all, which makes her admission condition all the more clear."

"We have a... complicated history," Brigitte said, fumbling a little. "We needed time... to move past our last encounter."

The woman stopped in her tracks and looked at them more closely. "You're that Parenteau kid, aren't you."

"I **was**." He felt the hair on the back of his neck raising at the reference, like he was Pierre's property. "I knew Celeste when we were kids."

"So you're the girl she attacked, then?" she asked suspiciously, her eyes narrowing slightly. "Are you **sure** Celeste is expecting you? I'd hate for her to suffer any setbacks."

Brigitte held up her hands. "I'd honestly hate for that, too. But the man at the desk said he checked, and she wanted to see us."

*I didn't think I'd ever see a time when anyone thought Celeste was fragile*, he said.

*I hope it's just a perception.*

He continued to be awed by Brigitte's capacity to forgive. It was something he aspired to master. He'd heard from Ruhul and Aalia, as well as a few other members of the class, about the horrible years of bullying and mistreatment his witch suffered at the whims of Celeste. But here she was, making an effort because Celeste was trying to be a better person.

The woman let out a hum but continued leading them down the hallway. She paused outside an open door. She knocked firmly, twice. "Miss Celeste, you have visitors. They **say** you are expecting them."

Celeste's voice issued out of the room. "Well, if it's Brigitte Defresne-Li and Tom Hēi, then yes, I am expecting them. Thank you Marjorie."

Celeste's room was bright and cheerful, with a mural of roses and honey bees on the walls. Her window that looked out into the large courtyard, walled on all sides by the rehab center. A place to

go outside without leaving the grounds. She had a dresser, a little
desk, a twin sized bed, and a bookshelf. It was probably the least
she'd ever had to live with. Beside the desk chair, against the wall,
sat a simple straight-backed chair that looked out of place, like it
had been borrowed from the dining hall or something. The dark
Siamese that had judged everyone along with her witch sat
attentive from the pillows at the head of the bed.

Hēi Māo stood in the doorway with his witch, feeling a little
awkward. How did you greet a long-lost friend who'd tried to hurt the
person who was most important to you? How did you reunite with
someone who nearly killed you?

Celeste was taller than Brigitte, but still several inches shorter
than him. Her build was closer to that of a contemporary model, but
her arms were more muscled than he remembered from their one
shared day of class. Her luxurious blond ponytail was gone,
replaced by a pixie cut. But the biggest change was in her face. Her
forehead was smooth, unfurrowed. Her blue eyes weren't
scrunched in judgment. She actually looked happy, something she
clearly hadn't been before her admission.

"Please come in," she said, waving them into her room. "You
can sit on the chairs, or the bed, wherever."

"It's nice to see you," Hēi Māo said, and it wasn't just good
manners prompting him. He'd been sad for the girl he'd gone on so
many imaginary adventures with.

Her smile wavered a little bit. "It's nice to see you, too. I
missed you, you know. I begged and begged to get to see you. I
knew what it was like to lose your maman, and I wanted to be there
for you." She shrugged. "I'm sorry you had to go through that
alone."

Brigitte took the least inviting chair, and Hēi Māo suspected
she was doing that thing where she tried to make everyone else as
comfortable as possible. There were emotional cues that he could

pick up from pheromones and scent, but Brigitte was so much better at reading the room. He took the other chair.

"You look really good, happy," Brigitte said. "It's nice to see."

"Thank you," Celeste said, her voice small as she moved to sit on the bed. "I... I actually didn't think you'd come. Either of you. I wouldn't have blamed you." Her eyes were shiny with unshed tears. She took a deep breath. "I'm so sorry for everything I ever did to you, Brigitte. I was so jealous."

"You were jealous?" Brigitte asked, clearly surprised. "Of **me**?"

Celeste sighed, her shoulders drooping. "People liked you without you having to do anything special, and I could never figure out how you did that." She let out a heavy sigh. "And your parents, no matter how busy they were with Nikli, they were always there for you. One or the other always showed up for school events and stuff. My papa was too busy to even have dinner with me most nights."

"That sounds horrible," Brigitte said.

"I'm not trying to excuse my actions, because I'm the one who chose to behave the way I did, but I'd like to explain if that's okay." Celeste met Brigitte's eyes uncertainly. "I think it will give my stupid choices some context."

His witch nodded. "If you think it will help me understand you better, I'll listen."

"*Mère* abandoned us, Papa and I, when I was five," Celeste explained. "I always thought it was **my** fault, that I wasn't a good enough daughter to make her stay." She shook her head. "It wasn't until I came here that I really recognized what it was I felt, and how wrong I was. My *mère* made her choice, I had nothing to do with it. She wanted a Hollywood career more than she wanted a marriage or motherhood, so she packed off to the United States without a warning or even a goodbye. I haven't heard from her since."

"Oh my gods," Brigitte said, horrified. "I can't even imagine how that must have felt."

"It didn't feel great, but it might not have been so bad if Papa's political career hadn't started to really take off right after she left," Celeste said. She gave a helpless little shrug. "He didn't physically abandon me, but I hardly ever saw him. When we were together, it felt like I was a prop or a tool to help him get elected. I had to behave in a certain way or present the right image. I couldn't be less than perfect. He was always too busy to play with me or read to me. We're practically strangers, and we're having to get to know each other all over again."

"I know exactly what that feels like," Hēi Māo said. "And I'm so sorry you had to go through that, too."

"Your father wasn't merely neglectful," Brigitte said with a growl.

"You're right," he agreed. "But a lot of the early stuff was very similar."

"Tom," Celeste said, her voice uncertain, and he realized it was the first time she'd directly addressed him by name. "If your father treated you that way, it's abuse. I didn't realize it until I came here. And you need to know that it's not right. It's not okay. Please trust me when I say that you need therapy."

"You're right," he agreed. "Mama suggested therapy after the whole Mademoiselle Butterfly demon thing, when I came out to the family." He'd initially thought Mama was suggesting it for Brigitte, since she'd been the one who ended up in the hospital. "And it's been..." Good wasn't the right word. Sometimes it was good. Other times it was incredibly hard. "It's been very helpful. But even with Dr. Wheeler, it took me... months to realize, or maybe accept that Pierre was abusive, and how he treated me gave me anxiety."

Celeste looked sad. "You didn't deserve that."

"I know that, **now**," he said. "And I'm in a much better place. I have a new family, and the best witch ever." He gazed at Brigitte until she blushed.

Celeste smiled. "She **is** a pretty amazing witch."

Even before she'd decided to visit Celeste, Brigitte had
needed to come to terms with her own feelings about the girl who
had been so nasty to her for most of her school life. When Lucie
delivered the first letter, the apology, back in November, she'd been
inclined to simply hope to never encounter the other girl again. But
during their Winter Solstice celebration, late in the evening when
she and Hēi Māo sat in the candle light and listened to music, they
talked about their childhoods. She'd shared her family's combined
Chinese and French traditions, visits with cousins from far away,
and her very favorite memories. He'd told her about the little blond
girl he'd gotten to slay dragons and conquer ridiculous puzzles with.
She couldn't help but wonder what had happened to turn Celeste
into the mean girl she knew.

When Lucie delivered the second letter, Brigitte realized she
had to find a way to work with Celeste. She didn't know why Celeste
had behaved the way she did, and she probably didn't need to
know. If Celeste wanted to do something that would help not just
Hēi Māo, but all the shape-shifters in Paris, Brigitte needed to find a
way to move past their history and let go of the hurt. They had a
shared cause, and though they might never be friends, that was
enough. It was a starting point.

Hearing about Celeste's childhood helped her let go of the last
bit of trepidation she'd been clinging to, the fear that this was all an
elaborate joke. She wouldn't necessarily trust Celeste. Not fully. Not
right away. But she knew she could work with her.

Over the course of their discussion, they'd all moved. They
knelt on the floor so they could look at the papers Celeste had
spread over the bed. "You've done an amazing job so far," Celeste

said. "All your public appearances have been sweet and completely non-threatening. Even to people who dislike shape-shifters. That means they'll listen to you."

"Thanks," Brigitte said, relieved to have another outside perspective. "I don't really know what I'm doing, and it's nice to know that I haven't completely messed it up."

"I'm not sure there's anyone who could have handled it better," Celeste admitted. Her fingers stilled over a spot early in the large timeline that sprawled over several pieces of paper taped together. "I'm not sure **how** you convinced Pierre to front Shift, but that was definitely a genius move. People see him as conservative, thoughtful and safe. The Parenteau reputation is solid and respectable." She paused for a moment, changing topic briefly. "Your designs, by the way?" She rolled her eyes up and raised her hands, wiggling them as though praising a higher power. "Fucking brilliant. I want them all, even the ones that won't look good on me."

Brigitte giggled. "Thank you so much."

"She's such an amazing designer, isn't she?" Hēi Māo asked, beaming at her from Celeste's other side.

"Yes, sweetie. I meant what I said," Celeste agreed. "Aalia's *Miraculous Morph* is very well done, too. It's professional, and I doubt anyone in Paris suspects it's being run by a *lycéen*." She looked slightly embarrassed, her pale cheeks pink. "I actually didn't realize it for the first three weeks, and I had to really dig to find information that told me it was Aalia's work. And it's only because I knew who she was that I figured it out."

"I thought you didn't have access to technology in here," Hēi Māo said.

"Oh, I have access," Celeste corrected. "It's just **very** limited. Because I've been doing so well, I've earned a little extra time, and I've been using it to learn more about shape-shifters in Paris, so I could figure out how I can help." She flapped one hand dismissively.

"I don't have enough time to get through all the things I want look up and read, and I'm not gonna waste what little time I have on chats and email."

"Wow," Brigitte said. She didn't ever remember seeing the other girl so invested in a project, any project.

"So you guys have already laid a really terrific groundwork for this. You've gained sympathy, and convinced a lot of people who weren't already invested in the anti-shape-shifter perspective." Celeste had apparently paid a great deal of attention to her father's previous few campaigns. She was also a whole lot smarter than Brigitte had given her credit for. She might be even more social media savvy than Aalia.

"We're starting this movement here, in Paris," Celeste said. "But in order for it to really have an impact, even here, this needs world-wide traction."

"Oh." Brigitte hadn't even considered that. Making Paris safe just helped her familiar and a small group of the shape-shifter population. And in order to maintain any success they earned, the mindset needed to be addressed beyond their borders. Their closest neighbors tended to influence policy.

"While I know you're the one who launched all this, you can't do it all." Celeste turned to face Brigitte, a totally serious expression on her face. "And I know you, Brigitte. You feel responsible for fixing this, even though it's an entrenched mindset throughout most of the world. You're going to try to manage everything, and you'll burn yourself out. I don't want to see that happen." She sounded painfully earnest. "Even if you don't want me involved, or if you can't work with me yourself, I'd like to help prevent that."

"We were **just** talking about this last week," Hēi Māo said, wriggling a little in his enthusiasm. "Brigitte needs to focus on the Butterfly side of things. It's getting attention, and we already have two high profile clients signed and waiting for bespoke Shift designs this summer."

Celeste's eyes went wide, and she looked like Solstice had come early. "You didn't tell me that! Oh my gods, congratulations!" She flung herself at Brigitte, hugging her tightly.

Brigitte found herself laughing, and unexpectedly hugging the other girl back. "Thanks."

Celeste straightened back up, making a show of getting herself under control. "Okay. Since you're already having success in that area, we need that to be your sole focus, okay? I bet I can send some other big names your direction, so we keep the momentum going." She snatched a checklist off the bed. "I know I've kind of fallen from grace, but I have a great come-back story planned, and most of my connections are still good."

Brigitte nodded. "What else do we need to be working on?" She realized Celeste's checklist was color-coded to match the timeline.

"We need to be bringing in more people, more voices," Celeste said firmly. "Aalia's doing some of that, getting shape-shifters and sympathizers involved. She's probably too busy to really pull off the full public relations thing right now, and I can't really wrangle that from here, but it's something that you need to be planning."

"Where can we start?" Brigitte asked, wondering what the bare minimum could be.

Celeste tapped at her lips with one finger. "Butterfly and *Miraculous Morph* both need a snapshot or digest type of social media. Yours should be photo-based, and Aalia's should be text. Make sure they're accessibility compliant. And if it's not too late, maybe an ally club or group can be started at school. The environmental movement has shown us that people our age and younger can make big differences."

"I can handle the Butterfly social media," Hēi Māo offered.

"Though if you could give me tips on top things to avoid as well as top things to include, that would be super helpful."

"I'll give something to Lucie for you when she's here next," Celeste agreed.

"Could we come back next week and talk more?" Brigitte asked. "I feel like you have a lot of great ideas, and I think I'm going to get overwhelmed if you share all of them at once."

Celeste froze for a moment, looking surprised. Then a soft smile appeared on her face. "You'd **want** to come back?"

Brigitte nodded. *I'm willing to bring her on board if you are,* she told Hēi Māo. She still didn't fully trust the girl, but she wanted to give her a chance.

"Could we bring Aalia, too?" Hēi Māo asked. "I think she speaks internet and public relations better than we do. And she might be able to help get things going until you're able to get more directly involved."

Celeste's face went blank and she swallowed uncomfortably. "Do you think she'd be willing to work with me? I mean… I was horrible to her."

"You were horrible to everyone," Brigitte pointed out. "But that was old Celeste. Unhappy Celeste. That's not who you are now."

"Thanks," Celeste said quietly. "If you can convince her to come, I'd be happy to try to make things right with her, too."

## Chapter Twenty-One

The third-floor sunroom of the Jeanne d'Arc rehab center looked out over the courtyard. Brigitte could see some of the center's residents visiting or playing in groups down below. The warm spring air flowed in through the open window, bringing the energy and growth of the season with it.

Ruhul and Aalia sat at a card table with Celeste, telling her about the recently formed shape-shifter alliance at L'Étoile du Nord. Monsieur Levale signed on as the adviser, and while they wouldn't be able to hold many meetings before the term ended, they were trying to establish regular meet ups for the coming summer. Exams were just around the corner, right after the upcoming Summer Solstice. *Première* progressive presentations would then take up the rest of the month before summer holiday.

Brigitte sat with Hēi Māo on a sofa near the windows while the others talked. She'd gotten so many things completed and off her to-do list in the last few days, and it was odd to have no urgent big deadline looming. The general calm made her constantly feel like she must be forgetting to do something.

She'd sent preliminary designs to Zara and Perci, and was waiting for their feedback and changes. They had meetings to discuss revisions next week. She really wanted to get both outfits completed well ahead of schedule, so she could focus on the next Shift release, something suitable for fall or winter. Or maybe something that allowed people to extend their wardrobe from season to season. Some of the designs already accommodated changes in the weather, but she hadn't fully explored that direction.

The excitement and fame that hit them at school after the fashion show, had worn off in the last few weeks. They had apparently managed to convince some of the undecided students that shape-shifters weren't anything to fear or hate. While there were now more kids who seemed supportive of Hēi Māo, and shape-shifters in general, the jerks were still jerks. And there were still too many who felt comfortable being nasty in a public setting. Ruhul's bullying report app continued to be used on an entirely too regular basis, and he'd suggested they consider contacting the school board with a summary of all their reports.

Brigitte tried to pay attention to Ruhul, Aalia and Celeste's plans. Knowing what they were working on was important, but she couldn't stay focused on the conversation. She'd had a couple of ideas involving magic and clothing that had been nibbling at the edges of her consciousness for days. She thought back to the discussion she'd had with Hēi Māo months ago, about triggering spells placed in a garment. She'd been too busy with Shift to focus on the idea, and now that things were calm again, it was back. She doodled, trying to nudge it out where she could really see it.

Beside her, Hēi Māo was doing exercises to work on his power awareness and control, something he'd been doing in a lot of his calm moments. His aunt Adalene's lessons and advice had been helpful, but Brigitte sensed that he was still worried about his destructive power. He still found it difficult to direct tiny amounts of his power, and preferred to aim for a person or thing's fortune when he wanted to have that finer control.

She watched as he held his palm open, the black sparkle of his magic lingering over his skin. He lightly placed a strip of paper in his hand, and it turned to ash. He took a deep breath and slowly let it out. Then he held up a similar strip of paper and poked it with one finger to destroy it. He still seemed comfortable, and she didn't feel him draw on her power for control at all, which was much better than his efforts at the same exercise a couple of weeks ago.

While letting her mind wander, she sketched the butterfly capelet that had gotten her so much notoriety. She drew out the wings, extended and fluttering like real butterfly wings. She stared at it for a moment, letting the idea fully form in her mind. While this was definitely not something she could mass produce for the general population, she definitely wanted to try it for herself. She'd seen video of people wearing glider suits instead of parachutes or hang gliders.

What would happen if she used magic instead of just relying on physics? "What if," she whispered to herself, "I could use magic to make actual flying wings?"

## *Chapter Twenty-Two*

It was a normal Tuesday morning, as normal as could be expected during exam week, any rate. Brigitte and Hēi Māo were eating breakfast, and trying not to worry about the day's tests. The sound of rushed footsteps outside the apartment broke through the intentional calm they'd established.

The door opened quickly, swinging into the wall with a bang, as Mama and Detective DuValle strode into the living room. Without realizing he'd moved, Hēi Māo had gotten up to stand between them and Brigitte. Everything about Mama was anxious, from the way her eyes darted around to the way she couldn't seem to stop moving. It was very clear where Brigitte's need to move in intense situations had come from.

"What's wrong?" Brigitte asked, finally getting up from the table and peeking around his shoulder.

"There's been an attack," Mama said, her dark eyes wide and watery, and he knew without a doubt she was remembering the loss of her familiar, Xīng.

"Why haven't we heard anything?" Brigitte turned to reach for her phone sitting silent on the table.

"The media's only just arriving on the scene," Detective DuValle explained. "At the moment it's a hostage situation. No one's been hurt, that we're aware of, though there is credible threat about explosives."

Brigitte slipped past him and went straight to Mama, catching both her hands and whispering soothingly to her.

Clearly the detective was here for a reason, so Hēi Māo started with the most logical. "Do they have someone we know?" He couldn't stand the thought of Aalia or Ruhul in danger.

Detective DuValle shook his head. "I don't believe so, but it is anti-shape-shifter motivated so it's possible. Right now we've only got one known terrorist making all the calls and demands. But it's been too quickly and too well organized to be orchestrated by one person acting alone." He pulled out his tablet, turning it toward Hēi Māo out to show him a picture of the old opera house, Palais Garnier. "The man is calling himself a French nationalist, which is a common line from xenophobes and ethnophobes who are opposed to a blended society. He says he's got a shape-shifter, just a kid, hostage, up in the top of Palais Garnier." He let out a sigh. "We've seen footage that tells us he does have a kid with him, and they aren't there voluntarily."

"Is the kid a shape-shifter?" Hēi Māo asked, then shook his head. "Actually, it doesn't matter." The kid could be a shape-shifter, an ally, or just some random person pulled off the street and used as bait. History had shown that hate groups would happily turn anyone into a target and twist the facts to fit their plan.

"He's demanding the mayor and the Council of Paris drop all plans to update statutes regarding shape-shifters. He's also demanding stringent penalties for failure to follow the current, and largely ignored French laws that designate shape-shifters as nonpersons and therefore ineligible to own property or vote." He seemed to think for a moment. "And his final demand is that Paris lead the rest of France in requiring registration for all shape-shifters."

Hēi Māo took a step back, horrified by those last two demands. "Registration of shape-shifters? So we can be gathered up and murdered?" He shuddered at the thought. Similar things had been done to other groups of people throughout history.

"He's threatening to toss the kid off the roof, and trigger a massive explosion if his demands aren't all met," Detective DuValle said.

Mama gasped at the word explosion, cringing in on herself.

"Since his demands are so extreme, there's pretty much no way that's happening," the detective said, "so we expect it to get tense and ugly, and there will likely be a detonation involved."

Hēi Māo frowned. He didn't care who this man was, he had no business upsetting his mama. He had no business threatening his people. "What can we do?"

"This is an all-hands situation. We're going out of the box and calling in reinforcements we don't usually use." Detective DuValle closed his eyes and sighed, the picture of resignation. "I've been sent here on behalf of the arcane branch of the Paris police force to petition for the assistance of Mademoiselle Butterfly in facing this threat." He held up his badge, and bowed his head, apparently presenting a formal request.

"What?" Brigitte asked, alarmed. "I'm a **designer**. How could I help? I have no training in dealing with this kind of thing."

"I advised against bringing you into this mess for those very reasons," Detective DuValle explained. "My superiors disagreed. We've all seen the report on how you handled that demon last fall, and the way you contained the vandals this winter was quite a follow-up. I felt if I were the one who came and talked to you, you could make your decision with complete information, rather than whatever tale the prefect of police told them to use." He tucked away his badge and his tablet.

"If I were to agree to help," Brigitte said, "what could I even do in this situation?"

"Brigitte, no," Mama said, a soft whine in her voice.

Brigitte patted Mama's hands, tucking the woman under her arm. "I haven't said yes, Maman. But I'm trying to get all the information I need. You raised me to help people. If there's anything I can do, you know I have to help." She turned back to the detective.

"We have a squad searching for the bomb, or bombs, because we have to suspect there could be more than one," Detective DuValle said, hooking his thumbs in his belt. "Once we've identified the uh, incendiary target, we can evacuate anyone living or working in the affected area. The metro and Paris bus is being held available for transporting civilians out. We'd then use magic to contain the blast, in the event that we can't prevent it from being triggered. That's where we'd like to use you." He glanced at Mama, then back to Brigitte. "The strength you exhibited back in October suggests that you could cast a ward that would contain the magnitude of blast this kind of group is capable of providing."

"How close would we have to get?" Hēi Māo asked. Perhaps distance would ease Mama's concerns. He knew Brigitte, and he knew where this was going.

Detective DuValle shrugged. "How far can you throw a spell?"

"We haven't actually tested that," Hēi Māo said. It was probably something they needed to do, to determine the range of both of their powers now that they were bonded. They'd been far too busy with their other projects to even think about it. Still, what they had done made it clear his witch went far beyond the norm.

He could feel Brigitte struggling to find a way to make her mama happy while doing what she felt she needed to. He bowed to

Mama. "Mama, you don't need to worry. We won't have to get that close."

"He's right," Brigitte said. "And I could protect others, people and familiars who might get hurt otherwise. I don't want anyone else to have to go through what you have."

"Are there others who could do this if we decline?" Hēi Māo asked.

Detective DuValle shook his head. "We have containment teams, but none are as powerful as Mademoiselle Butterfly. I hate to admit it, but having her help would make a huge difference. Far fewer people will be hurt, or die, if things go wrong." He sighed again. "And much though I wish it weren't true, this kind of situation almost always goes wrong."

Brigitte gave her Mama a tight hug before stepping away, holding her hand out to Hēi Māo. "Do we need to come with you now, or do we have time to prepare?"

"I can give you fifteen minutes," he said. "Change into something comfortable, and durable. I'll have ballistic jackets for both of you."

"Maman, I need you to go talk to Papa, and see if you have any potions that might help us right now," Brigitte said. "Boosters for health, mental clarity, strength, and good fortune." She nodded to the detective. "We'll go get changed."

Hēi Māo followed her as she charged up the stairs to their room. Without bothering with privacy, they both rushed to shed their nice school clothes. They would be warm, possibly uncomfortably so, in the thicker denim pants, but they were a safer choice. They picked soft light shirts to go under their police-issued jackets. He was still much faster, so while she was finishing, he went to her arcane tool chest to see what might be helpful. He pulled out two invocation sachets for each of the cardinal directions. He'd helped Brigitte make them during Summer Solstice, and they were very good to have in sudden need. There would be no time for candles and the niceties that went along with formal magic, which meant things could get out of control a little easier and the risk for backlash was greater. Offering something to the guardians could reduce that.

"Good idea, Kitty," she said, as she pulled her cat sling over her body. She'd modified it over the winter, adding a compartment to serve as a supply pouch. She could easily reach in and take what she needed, or he could pass things to her if he was already tucked inside.

"What else do you want?" he asked.

"A ball of black alpaca yarn, and the pouch of stones," she replied. "Yarn can be deceptively simple, but it can restrain so much."

He hadn't seen her use yarn in her magic, and he appreciated that she thought to mention that detail even now. He dug for the pouch of stones, then went to her yarn basket to find what she was looking for. "Need any knitting needles?"

She paused in the middle of pulling her butterfly capelet from its hook, then nodded. "Two. Wooden ones. I'm not sure yet what I'd use them for, but they could come in handy."

"Do you **need** the capelet?" he asked. Given that they would be wearing bulletproof jackets, it seemed unnecessary. He wondered if it was more for a sense of security.

Brigitte nodded. "We added spells to it, remember?"

He'd helped her with the magic just last week, but he'd been completely lost in the complexity of what she was doing. While she explained the steps, he hadn't been sure of the intent for everything she'd done. "Is there a shield?"

"There is." She buttoned the front of the capelet. "And the other is our emergency backup plan." She shrugged, shooting him a nervous smile. "Not sure how I feel about testing it today, but it's there if we need it."

He wasn't sure what that meant, but there wasn't really time to pry further.

Once everything was tucked into the sling, she went to their little sink and picked up the spray bottle they used to treat their clothes. "I'm dousing us both with this before and after we get those special jackets," she said. "Just in case."

"Too bad we can't fill a fire engine with that stuff," he said, hoping to lighten the mood. "We'd be able to protect a large area really fast that way."

"Remember that," she said. "We should revisit it when this is all over." She squeezed his shoulder. "You have good ideas too, you know?"

## Chapter Twenty-Three

Brigitte and Hēi Māo sat in the backseat of Detective DuValle's car. The world she knew felt like it had blurred into a surrealist image as he drove through the streets from Nikli toward Palais Garnier. His radio crackled with short bursts of words, code that made sense to those with training but left her utterly baffled.

*I know they say we'll be fine, but I can't help but worry this is bigger than they think*, she told Hēi Māo. *That when things go bad, it will be **really** bad.*

He squeezed her hand. *Great minds think alike. But it's not like we could stay out of this.*

She sighed. He was right. He'd known, before she even tried to make it clear to him that she couldn't back down from the official request for help. But this wouldn't be like the last time they faced something horrible. They had a small well-defined role and backup. Trained professionals were there to handle the really nasty stuff. She could make a ward, and stay out of the way.

*As long as we stay together, we'll be fine*, he insisted.

She nodded. She definitely didn't want to get separated from him in all this. She could have come by herself; all her magic training said she was just as powerful without him physically there, but she preferred having him by her side. She felt more confident in her magic with him present. If they needed to retreat behind her capelet, he could easily go into his sling.

Time was both weirdly stretched and compressed as the wide avenues of the second empire's reconstruction era all blended together. Eventually, Detective DuValle pulled to the side of Boulevard Haussmann to park behind a police car in a long line of emergency vehicles that stretched well up the road. He called something in on the radio that made absolutely no sense, then unbuckled his seat belt.

"Mademoiselle Butterfly, Tom, we're going to head up the block and take a right on Mogador Street. If we get separated, just get to the sidewalk in front of Galleries Lafayette, and I'll find you there. We'll get you two suited up, and find out if they've figured out where that bomb is."

The sidewalks were crowded with people in police, fire, and paramedic uniforms. Small groups stood around talking and pointing. The firefighters had gigantic ladders propped up against the Société Générale building and trampolines ready to go at a moment's notice. She held Hēi Māo's hand as they moved down the sidewalk. She didn't care if she got separated from the detective, and while she could always find her familiar because of their bond, she needed him within touching distance right now. She couldn't help but worry that she could lose him the way her mother had lost Xīng.

A few people glanced their way, but most were too busy with their own thing to bother with them. At least one man started to approach, clearly intent on sending them away, when Detective DuValle stepped in his path, one hand out in a clear signal to stop. She couldn't hear what he said, but the man backed off, surprise

172

clear on his face.

There were a couple of tables set up outside the Galleries Lafayette, and the people behind the table were distributing safety gear. Even from a distance the dark blue jackets looked heavy, probably oppressively so in the early summer weather. It didn't seem right that the sun was shining so brightly, and that the air smelled so fresh and sweet. Somewhere nearby, a kid was being tortured with the thought that they might die. A man was trying to use the threat of violence and harm to push his perspective. It was unfair that the world did not simply stop and acknowledge or respond to the horror in any way.

"I need gear for Mademoiselle Butterfly and her familiar," Detective DuValle announced when he reached the table. His voice had been loud enough to carry, and those nearest went quiet and turned to stare.

The woman on the other side of the table, looked over Brigitte and Hēi Māo before nodding. "Give me a small and a large," she called to her coworkers who sorted through bins of jackets. "The prefect want helmets on them?" she asked.

"She didn't say," Detective DuValle said, "but I'd prefer it."

The woman smiled, then ducked down to rummage under the table. She came up with two leather helmets, low profile, more like old race car gear than bulky motorcycle helmets. "Can you two try these on?"

Brigitte tugged Hēi Māo forward. "Thank you. I was hoping there would be something to protect my brain."

The woman laughed. "Grace under pressure, sweetheart. I like it."

Brigitte had to adjust the chin strap on hers a bit before it fit well. Hēi Māo's fit as it was. "How'd you get the sizes right on the first try?" Brigitte asked.

The woman smiled. "Never heard of sizing magic?"

Brigitte gawked at her for a moment. "There's such a thing?"

The woman nodded. "For something so small, it requires a pretty big power plant." She patted her chest twice. "But I've seen what you can do, and you should have no trouble learning it. When this is all over, Rogier can set up a meeting, and I can teach you. Sound good?"

Brigitte nodded. Sizing magic. It was a perfect fit for a designer.

"Thank you," Hēi Māo said, nodding to her.

They found a place out of the way, near the skyway that crossed over Mogador Street to connect the two buildings. While they waited to find out where they really needed to be, she and Hēi Māo made sure to spray their own clothes and the police gear they'd picked up. She wore her sling under the ballistic jacket, and the capelet over the top where she could use it if she needed it.

"It might not be enough to fully protect, especially if things get really bad," she said as she finished hitting his back. "I really made it for the kinds of things we might encounter at school."

"Better than nothing, Gitte," Hēi Māo said calmly. "Any extra buffer is good."

She couldn't help but worry about the things it definitely wouldn't be strong enough to matter for. "No getting crushed by falling buildings, okay?"

"Deal," he promised. "And if any try to crush me, I'll just toss some destruction at them."

That brought her a smile. "That's an excellent use for your power."

Detective DuValle trotted up to them as they were fastening their final snaps. "Okay, the bomb sniffers have found explosives rigged in two places. The first is over at Place de la République. It's a small one, and the daredevils who like to mess with detonators are already on site working through it."

Brigitte nodded. It was good news, but she suspected the second half of what he had to say might be less so.

"How big is the bigger one?" Hēi Māo asked.

"Terrifyingly big, actually," he admitted. "But I believe it's still within the scope of your ability to ward, and even if it can't fully hold it in, it won't be as destructive if we just let it go." He looked down the street toward Palais Garnier.

"He's planted the big bomb where he is?" Brigitte asked, shocked. If that were the case, he probably wasn't expecting to get out of this alive, which was definitely a worse scenario and would make things a lot more dangerous for the hostage.

Detective DuValle shook his head. "No. But nearby." He nodded toward the street that led to the old Paris opera building. "It's at Paris Le Grand."

Brigitte was vaguely familiar with the luxury hotel. It was one of the places Paris' more famous visitors stayed, but she wouldn't recognize it on sight. Outside of visiting the many nearby museums on school field trips, she hadn't spent much time in the ninth arrondissement .

She pulled her cell phone out of the jacket pocket and looked at a map, nodding once she was sure she knew where it was. "Has the hotel already been evacuated?"

"Under progress right now," the detective replied. "We're clearing the full two-block radius first, busing patrons out of the area. Then we'll move to empty the next two blocks around."

Brigitte reached through the pocket and into her sling for the pouch of stones they'd packed.

Detective DuValle gave her an odd look. "What have you stuffed in those pockets? They aren't that big."

Hēi Māo chuckled. He'd seen her modify the pockets while they waited for the protection spray to set.

"I ripped out the inside seam so I can get to my supplies." She unfastened the bottom few snaps of the jacket to show off the alteration. "I want the safety of the jacket, but I still need to reach my supplies. And if I end up carrying Hēi Māo in his sling, I want him protected by the jacket, too."

Detective DuValle shook his head. "You're an incredibly clever young lady, and I'm impressed with how well you've thought this through."

It was nice to hear. "Do you want me to prepare to ward the Paris Le Grand now?" she asked, tugging at the pouch strings to open it.

"What's it going to take for you to do it?" the detective asked. "Where do we need to be?"

"I can cast from here," she said. "It's well within my range. But the spell I want to use will require a few stones to be placed at these four corners." Holding the pouch in the same hand as her phone, she turned the screen to him and pointed.

The detective took a deep breath. "Do you have to place them yourself?"

Brigitte shook her head. "I'll need to charge them before giving them to whoever is going to place them, though."

He nodded sharply. "You charge them. I'll go get volunteers." He turned away, hesitated and looked back. "Do you prefer witch-born or not?"

"No preference," she assured him. She poured half of the pouch into her hand before passing it to Hēi Māo. "Help me find the onyx. They're black with white flecks and thin bands or striations. I need four of them."

Once she had all of the onyx she needed in her cupped hands, she let Hēi Māo deal with putting the rest of the stones back in their pouch. She closed her eyes and let the chaos around her melt away as she focused on infusing the onyx with her energy. She didn't need stones to create a ward, but it would be stronger this way. Likewise, the finished ward would hold better if the stones knew her and were prepared to link with her magic.

After several moments she relaxed. "Can you see or feel my magic on these?" she asked opening her hands to Hēi Māo.

He nodded immediately. "I can tell they're yours." He sounded a little surprised. "I thought that would take longer."

She shrugged. "Infusing them with my energy is a lot like simply being used in casting several times. It means my magic will find them more easily, bringing up the ward faster and making it stronger." She lightly stroked the onyx stones with her finger. "Onyx is good for protection, it can also be used in binding."

A few minutes later Detective DuValle returned, trailing three younger officers. "What do we need to do, to get those stones where you need them?"

*Can you hold these?* Brigitte asked Hēi Māo.

He held out his hands, nested together as a little bowl, perfect for this need.

Brigitte took out her phone again showing them the map, focused on Paris Le Grand. "I need each of you to place one of these onyx stones at one of these corners. It doesn't matter which one goes to which corner, but it would be good for all four of them to be placed at the curb." She switched the view from map to satellite and pointed. The placement would ensure that she had the entire building included in her ward.

"So just set them down, and that's it?" one of the officers asked. She nodded. "I can do that."

"I will need to touch each of you with my magic, so it knows you're working **with** me," Brigitte explained. "If this is okay, please hold out your dominant hand. If you don't want to be touched by my magic..." She stopped herself when she realized they were all holding out one hand. "Thank you for trusting me."

Holding up her left hand, Brigitte rubbed the tips of her fingers together several times, calling up just a hint of her power. She drew her fingers across each officer's hand, marking them with her magic. It was a temporary thing that would fade before she was even done casting the ward, but it would keep things properly aligned. With her right hand she selected an onyx stone for each officer, placing in their palm.

"You can close your hand, but please don't transfer it to your other hand if you can at all help it," she cautioned.

"We've all got radios, so the first one back will let you know when they're all placed," Detective DuValle said. "And we can let you know when the building is clear."

Once they were gone, she felt Hēi Māo's hand wrap around hers. The touch was grounding, comforting in the chaos. They didn't speak as they watched the professionals around them gather, then disperse to their positions. This wasn't the first big ugly crisis Paris had endured in Brigitte's lifetime. And while she'd always known there were a lot of people involved with minimizing harm, she hadn't realized just how many that entailed. Seeing such a large group dedicated to helping others, gave her a hopeful boost. Together they **could** stand against anything.

The woman officer was the first one back. She tapped the single ear phone plugged into her left ear twice. "The building is clear, but there are two stones left to place."

Brigitte looked around. Once the final stone was set she could begin, and she wanted a bit more space for that. "Where would be the best place for me to cast?"

How close do you need to be?" the woman asked.

"Oh, this is close enough," Brigitte said. "But I need to call up a circle to summon the magic."

The woman nodded, then ducked her chin to speak into her collar. "I have a witch-born who needs some space to call up a circle. We're just off the northwest corner of the intersection of

Haussmann and Mogador." She was silent for a moment and she looked up and around. "Copy." She gestured back toward Boulevard Haussmann. "We're just gonna go down the boulevard a little. I guess that's where we're staging all magic. You don't need to be able to see the Paris Le Grand to do your thing, do you?"

Brigitte shook her head. "Line of sight isn't needed for this." She and Hēi Māo followed the officer around the corner and up the street. From this new position, she couldn't see either Paris Le Grand or Palais Garnier due to other five and six story buildings standing between them.

There were a couple of other witch-born already using space in the street, some casting magic, others waiting. The officer led Brigitte to an opening between two actively working witches. "Here you go. I'm going to go back and make sure Rogier knows where to find you."

"Is he our chaperone?" Brigitte asked. They were by far the youngest people who'd been drafted to help.

"Essentially," the woman confirmed with a smile. "Good luck."

Brigitte took a brief moment to orient herself. Turning to face east, she slipped her hand out of Hēi Māo's to raise both of them skyward in supplication. "I call the guardians of the east, masters of harmony to keep this ward in tune with all other magics that must be cast today." She strode to the south, Hēi Māo trailing behind her. "I call the guardians of the south, masters of fire and will, to strengthen my ward and contain the flames of any explosion within." She moved to the west. "I call the guardians of the west, masters of water and purification, to douse any flames and contain any fumes so that our air remains untainted and safe." She walked to the north. "I call the guardians of the north, masters of stability and protection to build this ward strong enough to protect us today."

She reached out, and Hēi Māo placed his hand on hers. They walked to the center of her circle and he followed her cue to face north. During Summer Solstice they'd had plenty of opportunity to practice their workings together. She took a slow deep breath in, feeling him do the same. Then they spoke together. "We stand outside of time and place, on the threshold of never and always." She spoke the next part alone. "To ward Paris Le Grand, in the event that the explosives within are triggered."

Hēi Māo released her hand, moving to stand behind her with his hands on her shoulders. She closed her eyes and quested out with her magic feeling for and finding the onyx the officers had placed. Moving clockwise around the building she traced a line of magic connecting them. Then she raised her hands, bringing up a curtain of magic that surrounded the entire building. It would only be visible to those with magic sight. She returned her attention to the base of the ward, the sidewalk surrounding the hotel. She drew the magic down and around the concealed parts of the structure below street level.

Once the ward was complete, and the Paris Le Grand was contained within a sphere of magic, she let out a breath, slow and intentional. She opened her eyes and bowed to the north. "Depart in peace, elemental guardians. We humbly thank you for your aid."

*Well done*, Hēi Māo whispered into her mind. *Should you have a snack?*

This question, so basic and routine, made her giggle. "Yeah, I probably should."

He fished in the shoulder bag Maman had foisted upon him on their way out. The magical supplies had gone into Brigitte's sling, but the snacks stayed with him. He pulled out one of her favorite muffins, and handed it to her. "It's my job to take care of you, you know."

She was aware of the others around them, watching, but none of them mattered. Right now all she needed was the gentle care of her familiar.

## *Chapter Twenty-Four*

Once the ward was complete, Hēi Māo led Brigitte back to their original spot, making way for others to cast spells. Out of the way, they could see the back of Palais Garnier down the street. They had completed what they'd come to do, and Detective DuValle offered to see if it was possible to take them home, or put them on one of the outgoing buses.

"I'd rather we stay," Brigitte said. "In case there's something else we can help with."

"We're all charged up and ready to go," Hēi Māo added. After Brigitte had finished her ward, he started contemplating how he might use destruction in the same way. Could he create a bubble of destruction, like a Faraday cage, safe and contained on the inside, while the surface destroyed anything that tried to cross it? Having spent so much time assuming his power was misfortune, had taught him to consider how he could warp a negative into a positive. There was no reason he had to destroy **good** luck when he focused on someone's fortune. His aunt had found this line of thought too convoluted for her liking, but it made him feel better about carrying destruction. It helped him see the a constructive side.

There was a sudden up-swell of voices, as though hundreds had groaned all together. It came from the direction of Palais Garnier, and he couldn't help but look along with everyone else around them.

"Oh shit," Brigitte murmured next to him. She looked a little higher, so he followed her gaze and saw two people moving atop the the theater's flytower.

The outer edge of the peaked roof was flat, but narrow enough to risk a fall. Hēi Māo flinched and held his breath, worried that whoever was up there was about to drop over the edge. Any direction down was bad, as other roof lines jutted out from the side of the building, ready to catch a victim before letting them tumble to the ground.

The whole crowd of officers lurched forward down the street, and Hēi Māo's hand snapped out to grasp Brigitte's so they wouldn't get separated. As they grew closer to the opera house, he could see the man close to the edge waving something small in one hand. He clutched a fistful of his hostage's jacket as he jerked them around, their long blond hair loose and flopping about.

"How sure are you that your ward is gonna hold?" Detective DuValle asked, pushing through the crowd to face Brigitte.

"It'll hold," Brigitte insisted. "He's going to blow it up, isn't he?"

"He's definitely gotten less stable," Detective DuValle explained. "And that does make it a whole lot more likely. The bomb squad hasn't finished with the other one yet, so this building is going to have to be a loss." He let out a sharp exhalation that sounded like he was filling the space of a swear word he didn't think he should use. "I don't think he knows where the big bomb was placed."

"What do you mean?" Hēi Māo asked. Why wouldn't the man who was making the demands know?

"His words and actions have all suggested that he's expecting to serve time in prison, whipping his supporters into a frenzy from behind bars." The detective gestured to the roof. "But he's on the side of the building closest to Paris Le Grand. Nothing he's done makes us suspect he's witch-born, so it's safe to say he can't see Mademoiselle Butterfly's ward. He's waving that thing around, threatening to trip the bomb, like he's not concerned it's going to hit him, too." The man frowned. "He probably doesn't even realize he's not expected to survive this, that he's just a sacrifice to their movement, hoping to making him a martyr for their cause." He shook his head. "Fucking terrorists."

"What's in his hand?" Hēi Māo asked. "Is it a radio?"

"It's the remote for the bomb," Detective DuValle explained. "Or possibly for both of them. The recon folks said it's a dead man's switch; he has to hold the button or lever down, or the lack of signal will trigger the bomb."

Hēi Māo focused on the remote. He wasn't entirely sure how it worked, but he could feel its energy and he understood basic circuits. *I can fuse it,* he told Brigitte. *Melt the components so that it continues to send a signal even when he lets go.*

She looked at him in surprise. *Are you sure?*

He nodded. They had decided not to share shape-shifters' magical powers with the outside community just yet. They didn't need any other information to cause alarm.

"We can damage his remote," Brigitte told the detective. "Make it so that when he lets go of the switch, nothing happens. If he tosses it off the building or destroys it somehow, it will probably still trigger the bomb, though."

The detective held up one finger and muttered into the microphone at his collar. After a moment, he nodded. "Do it. We've got someone else who can protect it from damage once you're done."

Hēi Māo closed his eyes, focusing his energy on the remote. He wished he could trace the signal to the bomb, dealing with it directly, but that didn't appear to be a skill he had. Maybe no one did. He felt his destruction heat the solder, melting it and bypassing the switch to close the circuit. When he was done, he nodded.

"That should be taken care of now," Brigitte said.

"You two are full of surprises," Detective DuValle said, sounding impressed and pleased. "Let's get a little closer and see if you have any other bright ideas. I can't see things going well when that nutcase realizes he's lost his leverage of mass destruction."

It was hard, pushing through the crowd, and Hēi Māo realized he had a way to make it at least a little better. *Stop for a second*, he asked as he crouched down close to her feet. *Bend over me like you're gonna tie your shoe or something.* Either Brigitte had figured out his plan, or she simply trusted him to know what he was doing, because she immediately did as he asked without question.

He shifted, quickly climbing up her ballistic jacket to her shoulder. The fabric was stiff under his claws. As he'd expected, she was much better able to squeeze her way through small gaps of people on her own. Detective DuValle finally came to a stop on the sidewalk across the street from the opera house's flytower. Hēi Māo could see the man, wildly shaking his now defunct remote, though he was no longer holding on to his hostage.

In a very dramatic moment that caused the entire audience to flinch and gasp, he opened his hand, clearly releasing the trigger. He gazed out into Paris, expectant. Hēi Māo couldn't see his face from down here, but the man's body language gave him everything he needed.

There was no low rumble or bang of an explosion. He knew he'd been thwarted and all he had left was his hostage. He turned and stomped away from the edge for a moment only to return, holding the kid by their coat again.

The hostage was a girl, about eleven years old with blond hair. Hēi Māo let out a sudden horrified hiss as he recognized his cousin Iva.

"Fuck it all," the detective swore. "We don't have a solution for getting that kid down yet."

Without looking away from his cousin, Brigitte spoke. "If I have a solution, can I use it?" Her voice trembled, and Hēi Māo wasn't sure if it was fear or rage. She slid her fingers under the front of her capelet to unsnap the top two fasteners of her ballistic jacket.

Sitting on her shoulder, he could feel she was poised to act, her whole body tense, her magic waiting and ready to respond. He hoped that meant she had a plan to save Iva. He'd only just found his family, and he didn't want to lose any of them, especially not like this.

Detective DuValle stared at her for a moment, and Hēi Māo could totally relate to his awe. His Brigitte was a force.

"By all means, yes." The detective turned his chin to his mic and Hēi Māo's sensitive cat ears heard, the alert he sent out. "Be advised, I'm releasing the butterfly. I repeat, I'm releasing the butterfly."

Brigitte reached forward. "Sky and wind, aid me now as I enter your demesne." She grabbed at the open space to her right. "Fire, give me the freedom to change this situation."

The people closest to them backed off as her magic started to swell.

Without turning away from the crisis, she threw her left hand behind her head pulling it forward. "Water, grant me the freedom of dreams." Her hand shot out to the north palm up and fingers open before pulling a light breeze along with her fist. "Earth, give me strength in adversity." She reached behind her for the edges of her butterfly capelet, pulling it taut out to the sides. *Get in your sling,* she cautioned. *We're experimenting.*

That was all the warning he needed. Of course his Brigitte could fly. How else would The Butterfly save the day? He darted into her jacket, twisting around quickly so he could keep his head out the neck opening. *Let me know if you need anything.*

He couldn't see the fluttering of her wings, but he could feel them. With a little hop she rose into the air, moving far faster than a real butterfly. He felt his stomach drop as she twisted, rolling through the air.

Someone farther down the street had engaged the terrorist in an argument via bullhorn. Hēi Māo wondered if it was an intentional distraction. Planned or good luck, the man atop the flytower was so focused on the argument and terrifying his audience with his hostage, that he was apparently totally unaware of the girl flying toward him. He yelled angrily, inarticulate as he dangled Iva over the edge. Brigitte came in under Hēi Māo's cousin, close to the building. He hated that he couldn't do more to help either Brigitte or Iva, but all he could do right now was watch and wait, letting his witch use the boost he provided.

They shot up to Iva, the girl's light eyes wide as the man screamed in surprise. Hēi Māo found himself suddenly sandwiched between his witch and his cousin, as Brigitte snatched the girl away from the man, kicking off him to break away. The man staggered back and they were rolling through the sky again, arcing over to a building across the street. Brigitte found a relatively flat section of roof on the corner, and roughly landed them there. Her hand plunged into the one intact pocket she'd loaded with invocation sachets.

*Find me the yarn, then get out here to unbind Iva*, Brigitte demanded. As he ducked into the sling, he caught the distinctive scents of her invocation sachets bursting into flame, and he felt the elements instantly respond to her call. His claws dug into the ball of yarn, and he hauled it out the neck of her jacket with him.

As he dropped to the roof and shifted, he could hear screaming. The terrorist on the Palais Garnier seemed nearly ready to leap after Brigitte, though he clearly had nothing to help him with that. His witch, however, with her narrowed eyes and firm focus looked like she could kill the man and not care.

She unfastened the capelet and dropped it over his shoulders as he hunched over Iva. She was curled up on the roof, tightly wrapped in ropes full of magic. "Can I destroy these?" he asked, pointing to the ropes as he held out the black yarn. "Or will it backfire somehow?"

Brigitte held a hand over the ropes and took a deep breath. "They're high level bindings." She grinned at him. "No match for my kitty. Just be sure you focus on the ropes." She slipped a small knife out of her back pocket and cut off a length of yarn.

As Brigitte settled herself in an easy stance, Hēi Māo caught the knot between Iva's ankles. While his father had never quite done this to him, the binding felt similar enough and he hated it. He drew a slow breath, pushing aside his anger to gather up his power. When he was ready, he rubbed the knot with his thumb and forefinger. It fell apart, the rope rapidly turning to a trail of ash, like a cartoon fuse. After a moment, it was completely destroyed, and Iva lay limply, gazing up at him.

"I know you're not okay," he whispered. "And you might not be for a while, but Gitte and I are here for you. And we'll be here for you whenever you need us."

She crawled into his lap, her whole body trembling against him. It was probably shock. He remembered shock from his first aid classes, and he wrapped Brigitte's capelet more snugly around her.

Brigitte loomed over them, getting fully into the swing of her spell. "With air, I confine thee," she spoke, tying a knot in the black yarn. "With fire, I bind thee." Another knot.

He sensed something wrong, and his head snapped to the left

in time to see something flying through the air toward his Gitte. Without really thinking about it, he threw destruction at it, incinerating whatever the projectile had been. *We have company.*

"With water, I purify Paris from thy touch." She tied another knot. *Find them for me, if you can. I'm primed to bind more than one right now, and taking them alive will be much more helpful than the alternative.* "And with earth, I protect those who would be harmed by thy hate." A fourth knot joined the others. She held up the two ends, waiting.

*There's one on a roof down Auber Street, practically behind us and down a full block.* They were definitely witch-born. There was no other way they could have thrown a projectile so well from that distance.

"Got him." She tied the two ends together in a square knot "Upon cutting this yarn, let the binding dissolve. Blessings upon you guardians. I give thanks for your aid."

# Chapter Twenty-Five

Hēi Māo and Brigitte sat off to the side near the front of the great chamber, while the Council of Paris finished some of its regular business. It reminded him a little of their classroom, large desks for two councilors each in an amphitheater design, but much more opulent. These desks were cherry wood, with microphones and electronic voting switches on adjustable necks mounted along the top edge. What he could see of the walls was a soothing pale blue, thought they were mostly covered in faded cream and red tapestries. Being in the room helped Hēi Māo truly feel the age of their country. He had learned more about modern French and Parisian politics in the last two hours than in his entire academic career.

Fifteen minutes ago, he and Brigitte had been brought in from the comfortable waiting room where they'd spent the morning. Papa and Mama stayed behind, watching the live broadcast on the wall-mounted monitor. Their guide and handler wanted to be sure they were on hand and prepared when the council was ready for them.

Mayor Marchand firmly tapped his gavel against its striking block three times. "Our final two items of business are somewhat related." He beckoned, and the slight man who had been accompanying Hēi Māo and his witch quietly whispered for them to rise and step forward.

"First," he hesitated holding one finger aloft. "As unanimously agreed upon by this council, Paris shall bestow the Argent Ship Medal of Valor upon Brigitte Defresne-Li and Tom Hēi for their invaluable roles in apprehending French nationalist terrorists last week. The prefect of police has informed us that their aid prevented significant property damage and personal injury in the historic ninth arrondissement, including the anticipated total loss of Paris Le Grand and Palais Garnier. Their efforts ensured that the event resulted in no casualties and provided leads on the organization that orchestrated the event."

Mayor Marchand stepped forward gesturing for Brigitte first. As he placed the heavy medallion over her heart. "Thank you, Mademoiselle Butterfly, for your service to Paris at great personal risk to yourself and your familiar." He bowed.

His witch curtsied perfectly, something he'd heavily worked on with her in the last few days. When they received notification of the event, she'd panicked about what they would wear, then realized she had no idea how to address the mayor in a formal setting.

The mayor held out an identical medal hanging from a wide ribbon, striped in blue, white and red like the French flag. "Would you prefer to adorn your familiar?"

Brigitte glanced at him. *Do you want the mayor to be allowed to touch you?*

He thought for a moment. This wasn't something they'd even thought of. *I prefer to get it from you.*

Smiling, Brigitte reached out and took the medal. "Thank you for being considerate about this, sir."

As she pinned it over his heart, the mayor spoke again. "Thank you, Tom Hēi, for your service to Paris and your witch at great personal risk to you both." He bowed.

Brigitte stepped back once the medal was secure and Hēi Māo bowed low to the mayor.

Mayor Marchand turned to face the full council chamber. "Our next order of business is to vote on the repeal of the anachronistic statutes of Paris that are biased against shape-shifters." He puffed up his chest importantly. "It is widely known, and equally ignored, that Paris has had a large underground population of shape-shifters dating back before the French Revolution."

Hēi Māo hadn't been aware of this, but noticed that many of the councilors nodded along with the mayor's words. There were some who frowned, or sat back in their chairs, looking disinterested, but they were the minority. He wanted to be hopeful that appearances were representative of how the councilors would vote, but was frankly terrified of the outcome. What happened today would determine the future for his family, all the other shape-shifters he'd recently met, and so many others who were quietly living their lives avoiding suspicion.

"At our last meeting, it was decided that we would entertain final remarks before voting on the wholesale repeal of the selected statutes, rather than the time-intensive debate and vote on each individual statute." Mayor Marchand looked out into the room for a moment before continuing. "You have had the opportunity to discuss this with your constituents. And our recently decorated hero, Tom Hēi, has been granted a few minutes to speak to the repeal side of this issue."

Hēi Māo stepped up to the lectern, slipping his index cards out of his pocket onto the slanted surface. He reached out and adjusted the microphone for his height, then he nodded to the mayor, standing off to his right. "Thank you Mayor Marchand, and distinguished council members for allowing me this time." He took a deep breath. "We have all seen how nationalism harms the people of Paris," he said, leaning on all his past experiences of speaking on behalf of Parenteau. "Just last week we saw an innocent girl publicly tormented and threatened on the possibility that she was different. When we focus on difference, when we vilify those who are different, we damage our families and our culture." He was given such a short time to make his point, and there was so much he wanted to say. "My witch Brigitte is half Chinese. She and her mama get sneered at for not being French **enough**. They are French citizens by choice, which means they're far more dedicated to contributing to the culture and well-being of France than those who were born into it and have never bothered to choose."

He made sure to pan his focus across the room. "You may already know who I was before I met Brigitte and chose to become her familiar. In the event that you aren't aware, my mother went missing when I was very young. When this happened, I lost my connection to who and what I am. I'm French and Parisian, but there's more to me than that. And there was no way for me to seek it out, as shape-shifters can't safely advertise their nature to the public." It was time for his wrap up. "In school we are quick to chastise Americans for their treatment of Native Americans, yet what happens with shape-shifters in France is easily as horrifying."

He breathed slowly, focusing on getting these last words out clearly and confidently. "I ask that you correct a wrong that was done to a sub-group of French citizens long ago. Send a message to the rest of France and the world that this kind of intolerance has no place in a truly modern culture." He nodded to the council then turned and bowed to the mayor. He moved back to Brigitte's side and walked with her off the podium, following their handler back to the waiting room.

## Chapter Twenty-Six

Hēi Māo ran through his *première* progressive one last time, looking for typos and awkward phrases. His appeal for a later time had resulted in him getting the very last presentation slot on the last day of school. Who could have guessed that finals week would end up changing his entire plan for this huge project? Instead of a summary of what he'd learned in his seven months at L'Étoile du Nord, with a focus on social skills and knowledge gaps, he would be sharing how he'd gotten to know himself in the last year. He'd left out some of his reasons for running away from home, not convinced that he wanted the world to know how abusive Pierre was just yet, if ever. The defining moment, and focus of his presentation, wasn't rescuing his cousin from a terrorist, but helping make Paris safer for shape-shifters.

The hum of Brigitte's sewing machine provided a comforting background as he worked. Her presentation had been that afternoon, and had been very well received by students and teachers. Things were gradually returning to the normal he and his witch had established. They had three more days of *première* progressive presentations to get through, including Aalia's, then the school year would be over. They'd have all of summer break to work on Brigitte's next line and explore new things.

"How's it going over there, Kitty?" Brigitte asked as she pulled her project out of the machine, clipping its tethering threads.

"Nearly done," he said. "It's a lot better than my other one, so I'm really glad I petitioned for a new presentation date."

"May I read it yet?" she asked, the sound of flapping fabric accompanying her words.

"Soon." He wanted her feedback once it was really ready, and he was definitely hoping to make her proud. He looked up to see her shaking out a new butterfly capelet, this one had the white-outlined, dusty-blue wings of an Amanda's blue. It was a little smaller than her capelet, sized to fit Iva, likely for a couple of years. "Oh that's gorgeous," he whispered. "She's going to love it." He pushed against the floor with his feet, propelling himself slowly toward her. "Is it done?"

"The sewing is," Brigitte said. "If she's okay with it, I'd like to spell it for protection and shielding like mine. I think having something like that will help her feel safer."

He nodded. His cousin hadn't returned to school, and her final exams had been waived given the circumstances. She'd barely left home since her abduction. His aunt said she was doing better every day, but that her therapist said it would be a long recovery. The Defresne-Li apartment was one of the few places she'd been willing to go without an argument, cajoling, or tears.

"I think she'll want that extra protection," he agreed, "but it's a good idea to let her make that decision." Giving her control over anything they could felt like the right choice right now. It was one of the things Brigitte had done for him that had made such a difference when she'd first brought him home as a stray cat.

"When are we expecting them?" Brigitte asked, continuing to

look over the seams and appliques to ensure they were finished properly.

"Any..." He hesitated as he heard footsteps on the stairs to the apartment. "Now, actually." He grinned and moved for the stairs down from their room. "I'll go let them in." He reached the door at the first knock.

"Good evening Hēi Māo," his aunt said, leaning over the grocery bags in her hands to greet him with proper *bise*. Since this was one of the few places Iva was willing to go, and her therapist wanted her getting out of the house as much as possible, they'd been coming over every other evening. After the first few days, they had started bringing dinner or the fixings for it. The last few visits, they'd coordinated with Mama and Papa on bread and dessert.

"Good evening Auntie Adalene, Uncle Marcel," he nodded to his uncle. He stepped back to let them in, and looked around them for is cousin. "Where's Iva?"

Marcel looked down at the front of his light jacket, that it was definitely too warm for, and shook his head. He unfastened the buttons to show a sling holding a black kitten. The tiny ragged purr was clearly a self-soothing mechanism.

"Rough day?" Hēi Māo asked, wincing a little.

"That'd be a spectacular understatement," Marcel agreed.

Hēi Māo closed the apartment door and locked it, knowing both those steps helped her feel less threatened. "Hey Iva, I hope you're willing to come out of there. Gitte has something really special for you, but it's way too big when you're in cat form."

Iva peeked out of the sling, her ears pricked and her eyes wide.

"C'mon Kitty-girl," Hēi Māo said. "You know you're safe here, and upstairs is a lovely refuge for you." From his own experience, he knew logic couldn't always defeat the demons of anxiety and fear, but it was a good place to start. "But I want you to do what you feel you need, okay?"

She rested her chin on the edge of the sling for a moment before tentatively reaching one paw out for him. He tickled her paw pads with one finger and she batted at him, her eyes scrunching up in annoyance.

"Do you want to go up on your own or should I take your papa's sling?" Hēi Māo asked, wanting her to choose if she could.

Iva let out a huff before slithering out of her sling and dropping gracefully to the floor. She shot up the stairs.

Hēi Māo smiled and followed her. "Let us know when dinner's ready."

"We will," Marcel promised. "And let us know if she needs anything."

Brigitte was accustomed to cats darting around the house. Even before she brought Hēi Māo home, Callie had been known to dash around or through rooms she'd been in. Hēi Māo did it too, and he'd explained, back when she thought he was just a cat, that it served two purposes. The first was that it was fun, and really that could have been enough. The second had to do with burning off pent up energy to keep the fidgets to a minimum. The more active he was throughout the day, the less he needed to zoom around the house.

She could always feel Hēi Māo's approach. Callie's feet made enough noise to forewarn her. Iva, however, was so little and light that she tended to catch Brigitte off guard. She let out a surprised squeak when a black kitten dashed into the room. She ran a circuit, taking advantage of the landing and launch spots Brigitte had set up with Hēi Māo's help. She smiled, happy to see his cousin comfortable enough to freely be herself here.

"It's good to see you, Iva," she said. She giggled when the

little black blur veered off her current path to land in Brigitte's lap, plowing against her stomach with a grunt. Brigitte ran her hand over Iva's silky fur over and over again. "I'm so glad you're here."

"I guess we know who Iva-kitty's favorite person is," Hēi Māo said, as he stood at the top of the steps. He tipped his nose in the air. "Frankly I'm hurt that it's not me, but I must admit she has excellent taste in witches."

Iva turned toward her cousin and blepped at him.

Hēi Māo gasped in mock horror. "Such sass!" *Where's her gift?* he asked, glancing around Brigitte's work space.

*Gift bag behind the changing screen,* she told him. She'd planned on drawing it out, but maybe that wasn't the best idea for today. "Did Hēi Māo tell you I have something for you?"

Kitty Iva nodded, then nudged Brigitte's hand for more petting.

Chuckling, she complied with the obvious request. "Well, when you're ready for it, you'll need to shift, because it will require fingers."

"Fingers are the best part of being a shape-shifter," Hēi Māo said happily. "All the benefits of being a cat, plus fingers." He wiggled them vigorously in Brigitte's direction as he went to retrieve the reusable cloth gift bag from its hiding spot. Once he had it, he sat down on the chaise, careful not to crowd his cousin. He crinkled the tissue paper a little, clearly teasing Iva.

"And what are all these cat benefits you speak of?" Brigitte asked. "I need to know what I'm missing out on here."

"The cuddles and pats are nice, of course," Hēi Māo said. "But the best thing I've found was this super amazing witch."

"Really?" she demanded. He was being a silly kitty.

"Really," he insisted. "She let me keep her as my very own witch, you know. Totally transformed my life." He beamed at her. "Best. Witch. Ever."

Brigitte burst out laughing. "Silly kitty." She gave his shoulder a gentle push. "But you are the best familiar ever, and I'm not biased. I know what I'm talking about."

"May I give you pets, too, Iva?" he asked. "I don't have to, if you prefer just Brigitte's touch. But I want you to know I'm here for you, too."

Iva let out a couple tiny half meows before slowly moving off Brigitte's lap to sit between them.

"Thank you, Kitty-girl." He rubbed his fingertips behind her ears and under her chin. Brigitte paid close attention, knowing that he was more aware of all the best spots for scratches.

"I'm glad you came to see us even if you're having a rough day," Brigitte said. "Sometimes finding a little bit of normal can help get you through the tough spots."

After a few more minutes, Iva stretched out, gradually reaching off the chaise for the floor. Then she hopped down and shifted in a flash of green light very much like Hēi Māo's shift.

Iva sat cross-legged on the floor, dressed in a ratty t-shirt and shorts that were clearly from last summer. Her hair didn't look like it had been brushed since her last visit. Brigitte had learned that while changes in grooming habits could be a warning sign for anyone, they were especially critical for cat shape-shifters.

"You look like you feel awful," Brigitte said softly. "A little home spa experience might help. Can we please try?"

Iva let out a huge sigh and nodded, her eyes trained on the floor.

*Get the brush and comb. You're on hair,* she told Hēi Māo. He'd proven remarkably good at doing her hair. "When you're ready, you just settle yourself up on the chaise, okay?" She went to her desk and paired her phone with their music system. "First up, spa music," she said dramatically. The meditation playlist Ruhul had made for them poured out of the speakers. She adjusted the volume so it was appropriately background.

Halfway up the ladder to their bed, Hēi Māo snatched his kneading blanket, the square of soft loose knit he'd made for his own stress relief. He hopped down and dropped it into Iva's lap. She'd managed to move to the chaise faster than Brigitte expected, so that was a positive sign.

"Knead that," he suggested. "Just squeeze and squish it. Trust me, it helps." Then he went for their brushes.

From the sink in the corner, Brigitte filled a basin with warm water. She pulled a bottle from her supplies and dripped some mint oil into the basin. In short order, Iva was soaking her feet and relaxing under Hēi Māo's gentle brushing.

Brigitte ducked downstairs briefly for some tea, a soothing concoction Maman had started making for Hēi Māo over the winter. She assured Adalene and Marcel that everything was fine, and there was no need to disrupt their dinner preparations. It was nice to see how smoothly her family had expanded to include Hēi Māo's supportive relatives.

Back upstairs, she set Iva's tea on the tiny table they'd moved nearby, then delved into her knee-wall storage space. Hēi Māo's cousin was taller than she'd been at eleven, but no where near her current height. She sorted through a few things before pulling out a bin. Appearance could reflect mood. But it could also influence it.

"I know that's probably a comfortable shirt, but the same can't be said about those shorts," Brigitte said. "Let's see if we can find you something else to wear."

Iva nodded. She was often silent during their visits.

"I realize my style isn't necessarily yours, but..."

"That's okay," Iva said quietly. "I... I don't really feel like myself anymore." She frowned. "I mean... I feel like a different version of me. I'm still Iva Barbeau, but..." She sighed again.

"That makes a lot of sense," Hēi Māo said as he styled her hair. "The me I am now is very different from the Jacque Parenteau who ran away from home a little over a year ago. I'm still me, but I'm not the same."

Iva nodded, a small smile of relief on her face. "Yeah. It's like that. Only… it happened all at once and it wasn't my idea at all."

"It's hard when life changes you without your permission," Hēi Māo said, setting aside the brush and comb he'd been using. "But I know that we love the new version of Iva just as much as the old one." He rested his hands on her shoulders and leaned forward to peer, upside down, into her face.

"I hardly know who I am now," she complained.

"Can we help you try to figure that out?" Brigitte asked. "And if you're not entirely happy with what you learn about new you, you're allowed to reinvent yourself as much or as often as you need to." She pulled over her office chair.

"Everyone else is trying make me who I was before I got kidnapped," Iva blurted, then she shook her head. "But I can't be that girl anymore."

"Is that what your therapist is trying to do, too?" Hēi Māo asked, his face concerned.

"Not really." Iva shrugged. "She's trying to help me feel safe like I used to, but… I guess she hasn't really said I should try to **be** the same again. It's just that it feels like that's what she's saying."

"I think we should talk to your parents about this," Brigitte said. "I know they want to help you, and letting you explore this in your own way might do that." She tapped the bin. "But for now, let's see if any of my old clothes seem like something you think new Iva would wear."

Her smile was tentative. "Yeah. Okay. Let's do that."

When they escorted Iva down to dinner, the front of her hair had been pulled back from her face in a little braid that rested on top of her loose hair in back. She wore a black sleeveless dress that had been Brigitte's first experiment with stretch crepe

Georgette fabric, and it had been a favorite until it got too short. Over her shoulders she wore the Amanda's blue capelet, now infused with magic to prevent stains and to protect her from harm.

"Oh, you look so nice," Maman said, stepping away from the table she was setting. She beamed at Iva. "I remember when Brigitte made that dress. It suits you."

"Thank you Auntie Ling," Iva said. Again, her smile was small, but it looked real, and Brigitte was glad she'd found at least a little happiness today.

Maman lightly patted Iva's cheek. "Did you know she's gotten hundreds of requests for butterfly capelets? But they won't be available to most people until her next release in September."

"You have to be pretty special to be a butterfly," Papa agreed. "What kind are you?"

Iva spun in a circle, letting the capelet flare out around her. "I'm an Amanda's blue. They're my favorite."

"Good choice," Papa said. "And is our Amanda's blue ready for dinner? We have some of your favorites for today."

## *Chapter Twenty-Seven*

Brigitte stood with Aalia at the bottom of the steps in front of L'Étoile du Nord while Hēi Māo raved about Ruhul's presentation, which had been held only a few students before his own. In the end, all of their *première* progressive projects had been influenced by her familiar, something she never would have expected when she first brought him home. All of them had changed their plans halfway through the year, or later. Ruhul's work on the Shift release show soundtrack had sparked his interest in studying the art and science of music's ability to influence emotion and reaction.

"Easy there, Cat-dude. You're going to embarrass me." Ruhul chuckled, his hand going up to rest on Juniper's rump, as if she needed help balancing on his shoulder. She poked her nose into his hair and shook her head briskly, disrupting his curls.

"But it's so cool, now that I can see it," Hēi Māo insisted. "Pierre never works directly with the audio production team for any of his shows or after-parties. That's all on the marketing department."

"Someone there probably knows what they're doing," Ruhul

202

said with a shrug. "Or they've got good taste and good luck."

"Are you two both still up for tomorrow?" Brigitte asked. They'd had to surrender their Friday game night this week to tradition. Most families celebrated the end of the school year with dinner or a small gathering.

"Yes, and looking forward to it," Ruhul said. His extended family was taking over his uncle's Moroccan restaurant in honor of all the cousins who finished school today. "It feels like forever since we've gotten a full day together that didn't somehow involve one of our projects. It'll be a nice way to start the summer."

"It really has been a while," Aalia agreed. "I may take a few pictures tomorrow so I remember what to come back to later, but I'm not doing any reporting or research."

"Wow," Brigitte said. "You're really committing to this relaxing thing." She grinned when her friend gently swatted at her shoulder.

"We are showing our favorite cat some of the treasures of Paris," Aalia said, giving the blond a smile. "I want to make sure I'm focusing on that, not my next scoop."

"Thanks," Hēi Māo said. "You guys are really the best friends I could have ever gotten. I feel super lucky to have you in my life."

Ruhul tilted his head and held out his arms. "We're gonna have to hug you now. You know that, right?"

Hēi Māo sat on a floor cushion between Iva and Brigitte, nibbling on after-dinner sweets in the living room. As the guests of honor, they had been forbidden from helping clean up. Mama, Papa, Auntie Adalene, Uncle Marcel, and Master Fu chatted as they made quick work of the leftovers and wash up. They had invited Pierre, but no one was surprised when he declined, citing schedule conflicts. He had unexpectedly sent over flowers and very nice fountain pens for all three students.

"You seem to be having more good days than bad," Hēi Māo said, looking at his cousin. She was wearing another of Brigitte's old cast-off outfits, and it seemed like most of her wardrobe now came compliments of his witch.

Iva nodded, swallowing the bite of strawberry macaron she'd been enjoying. "I am. It's nice."

"I'm really glad to hear that," he said. "If there's anything we can do to help you maintain that, let us know, okay?"

Iva took a deep breath. "I think I might be ready to go thrift shopping?" Her voice was uncertain as she looked at his witch.

"Excellent." Brigitte looked pleasantly surprised by this news. With commissions and preparations for the fall Shift release, she couldn't make all of Iva's clothes, though he was sure she would have offered. His cousin was still experimenting with her new look, so thrifting made the best sense.

"Probably not on the weekend," Iva cautioned. "I'd rather avoid the stupid big crowds if I can."

Brigitte nodded. "That makes excellent sense. We can start with one place, and if you just aren't feeling it, we'll come right back here."

They'd offered to have Iva over twice a week over summer break so Marcel could go back to work part time, at least as an experiment. His job was willing to extend his leave further, but Iva's therapist had suggested trying to move back toward a more routine schedule as much as was tolerated.

The adults slowly drifted into the living room, settling on the couch, chairs or floor cushions.

"I am so proud of all of you," Mama said, reaching out to give each of them a quick hand squeeze. "You all faced challenges you weren't expecting this year, and you've handled them with such strength and poise."

"And you all have summer plans that will help you move in a

positive direction," Papa added as Callie moved to his lap. "You'll be returning to school even brighter than you are now."

"Thank you, Maman, Papa." Brigitte beamed at her parents. "You know we couldn't have done half of it without your support."

"None of you are the same person you were when you started school in the fall," Auntie Adalene said, catching their attention. "And I'm enjoying getting to know you all over again." Hēi Māo was impressed with how well his aunt had taken Iva's self-exploration.

Iva lurched forward to hug her mother.

"I'm grateful to have all of you in our lives," Uncle Marcel said, nodding to each of them as he continued. "Lost family, found family, and friends alike."

Master Fu smiled, and Hēi Māo felt the room grow more calm. "You two have come so much farther than I'd ever imagined." He held his hands out to Brigitte and Hēi Māo. "And I've never seen a more perfectly matched witch and familiar pair."

Hēi Māo felt Brigitte's pleasure at that. "Your training has helped me be the familiar I am." He liked including Master Fu as found family, a concept that was new and terribly appealing.

Master Fu nodded. "I'm afraid Adalene will have to take over your training for the next few weeks, as I must take another trip."

Hēi Māo smiled at his aunt before turning back to his primary mentor. "She's helped a lot, too. Especially with the nature of my magic."

"Is it another workshop or conference?" Brigitte asked.

Master Fu slowly shook his head. "No. This is something else all together." His gaze settled on Hēi Māo. "I've told you I knew your mother well, but I left out how we met." The room went unnaturally silent. "Ysabeau and I were heavily involved with the Shape-Shifter Railroad. She disappeared during an afternoon escort that was considered a very low risk."

Hēi Māo swallowed nervously and nodded. Brigitte's arm slid

around his waist and she caught his near hand in hers. Though it wasn't as bad as the first time he'd learned Master Fu was friends with his mother, his head felt full of static.

"While we can't be certain of anything yet," Master Fu continued, "I have reason to believe that Ysabeau is being prevented from returning to France against her will."

"If Wang can find where she is," Adalene said, her voice full of promise, "we will bring her home."